Some Haunted Houses of England Wales

Elliott O Donnell

ISBN: 978-93-6144-032-8

Publisher: **Neelkanth Prakashan**

Address: 4760-61, 23, Ansari Road,
Daryaganj, New Delhi-110002
Phone: 9810675061
WhatsApp: +91 9810675061
E-mail: neelkanthprakashan47@gmail.com

Edition: 2024

Printed By: Gupta Communication Shahdra 110032

Some Haunted Houses of England Wales
Elliott O Donnell

Table of Contents

PREFACE

IN selecting a series of ghost stories for this volume I have taken the greatest care to make use of those only which are thoroughly well authenticated.

The result of this discrimination has been that the majority of these accounts of psychic phenomena have been taken from the lips of eye-witnesses and transferred to manuscript in as nearly as possible the narrator's own language.

First-hand narratives of unfamiliar hauntings, albeit they refer to the meaner class of houses, will, I think, be more welcome to the reader than the mere repetition of such hackneyed stories as those appertaining to Glamis Castle, the Tower of London, &c.

In one other point, too, this work may be said to differ from others dealing with the same subject—viz., it is compiled and written by a very keen psychic—one who has not only investigated (and lectured on) haunted houses, but has himself seen many occult manifestations.

As there have been several libel cases quite recently in connection with the alleged haunting of houses, I have been obliged (save where it is stated to the contrary) to give fictitious names to both people and localities.

ELLIOTT O'DONNELL.

GUILSBOROUGH, NORTHAMPTON.

HAUNTED HOUSES

THE GREEN BANK HOTEL, BARDSLEY

THE RACE FOR LIFE

Technical form of apparitions: Phantasms of the dead

Source of authenticity: Evidence of eye-witness

Cause of haunting: Murder

ONE afternoon in the July of this year I took tea with Lady B—— at her club in the West End. Lady B—— is a very old friend of mine, our friendship dating back to the days when I wore Eton collars and a preparatory school cap. She was in unusually high spirits at the thought of a cruise in the Baltic, whilst I was equally exuberant at being once again in London after a very trying sojourn in a particularly remote and isolated town—a town renowned for pilchards, pasties and Painters.

Now, there is nothing mean nor petty about Lady B——; she is generosity itself: so kind, so courteous, and withal so daintily pretty that to be near her, even, is to be in Elysium.

Remembering the interest I had always taken in matters psychical, she had invited several friends especially to meet me, and it was from one of them—Miss Charlotte Napier—that I heard the following story:

"Chancing to be stranded late one night at Bardsley," she began, "owing to a slight miscalculation of the time-table, I had no other resource than to put up at the Green Bank Hotel in Russell Street.

"It was a very ordinary hotel; ordinary both in accommodation and appearance. One part of it—that in which I slept—possibly dated back to the Elizabethan period, but the rest—most hideously renovated—was quite modern.

"Outside my room—No. 56—was a long and somewhat gloomy corridor connecting the old and new portions of the house.

"I retired to rest about eleven—closing time—and had been asleep barely an hour before I awoke with a start to find the room flooded with a pale, phosphorescent light.

"The moon shone through my window-panes: it gleamed with an unearthly whiteness across the bed, and thence across the room, glancing upon the panels of the door in such a manner that I was constrained to follow its course and to fix my gaze wherever it shone.

"The door was a mass of light: I could see each crack and scar upon it, even the finger-prints on the white handle, with painful distinctness. A sudden sensation of horror overcame me; I would have given anything to have been able to look elsewhere. I could not.

"All my senses were centred upon the door; it enchained, it drew me, and as I gazed at it in helpless awe the sound of footsteps from without suddenly broke upon my ears. Instantly all my faculties were on the alert, and I became the victim of a curious sensation unlike any I had hitherto experienced, but which I have since learned is the usual effect of psychic manifestation. I felt the proximity of the unnatural. An icy coldness stole down my back, my teeth chattered, my hair seemed to rise on end, and the violent palpitation of my heart made me sick and dizzy. My faculties had indeed become abnormally acute, but my body seemed no longer alive, and I knew that whatever happened I should be absolutely incapable of action. My powerlessness was soon to be put to the test. Sitting bolt upright in bed, in obedience to an irresistible impulse, I listened, listened with all my might. What were those sounds? They were certainly unlike any I had ever heard before, and the kind of terror they imparted was hitherto unknown to me. Perhaps the nearest semblance to the kind of fear I then felt is the fear inspired by the sight of a lunatic. I could not stir, I could only wait and listen. The unnatural nature of the footsteps was emphasised by the brilliancy of the moonlight—quite an abnormal feature in itself—and the intense hush, which, stealing surreptitiously upon the house, obliterated every other sound.

"The footsteps gradually became interpretative—two people were rushing headlong down the corridor!

"From the light, flying footsteps of the foremost, and the heavier tread and ever-increasing pace of the hindermost, I concluded it was a race entailing vital consequences, and that the fugitive would soon be caught. Caught! but not, pray Heaven! at my door.

"What on earth had happened? What could happen in a well-regulated hotel?

"Fire, robbery, or murder?

"MURDER! Great drops of sweat broke out upon my brow at the bare thought.

"The moon shone in, whiter and more coldly than ever, whilst the steps drew nearer and nearer—so near, in fact, that I fancied I could detect the sound of breathing. Short, sharp-drawn gasps of agony accompanied by easier and more strenuous inhalations.

"Who were the actors in this invisible drama? Were they both men? I imagined not! Indeed, a thousand horrible ideas suggested themselves to my mind—to be interrupted by a terrific crash on the upper panels of the door that made me all but die with terror. Never had I suffered as at that moment. I strove to scream—it was in vain; my tongue clave to the roof of my mouth; I could utter no sound.

"The door (which I had taken the precaution to lock) was unceremoniously burst open, and into the room rushed a very young and fragile looking man clad in the costume of a Cavalier of the time of Naseby, whilst close at his heels there followed a gigantic Roundhead armed with all the terrible paraphernalia of war.

"The tableau was so totally different from anything I had anticipated, and withal horribly real—so real that had it been in my power I must inevitably have raised a hand to interpose.

"Indeed, the wretched fugitive made straight for my bed, and, falling on his knees beside it, clutched the counterpane convulsively in his fingers. His ashy face was so near mine that I not only saw every feature in it with damning clearness, but I read the many varied expressions in his eyes.

"They were awful. I read in them despair, terror, hate, overshadowed in the background by an insatiable craving for every imaginable vice.

"Yet they were beautiful eyes—beautiful both in formation and colour—too effeminately beautiful for a man.

"His hair, which fell in a wild profusion of ringlets over forehead and shoulders, was of a rich chestnut hue and most luxuriant.

"He wore neither beard nor moustaches; he was absolutely clean shaven, and his skin shone with all the milky whiteness of that of a young woman.

"His features were neatly moulded and extremely delicate; his hands well shaped and narrow, whilst his fingers, long and tapering, were crowned with pellucid filbert nails.

"Attired in the most costly and elegant manner, a manner that suggested the court fop rather than the soldier, he formed in every way a marked contrast to his puritan pursuer. The Roundhead was a huge, brawny fellow, dressed in a leathern jerkin and heavy riding-boots—his soiled and muddy clothes betokening the wear and tear of an arduous campaign.

"His face, always ugly, and naturally, perhaps, sullen and forbidding, was now positively diabolical; rage, hatred, and triumph vieing with one another for supremacy.

"Catching hold of the Cavalier by his silken tresses, and pulling back his head by brute force, the Cromwellian slowly and deliberately drew the keen blade of his knife across the doomed man's throat.

"The horrid deed—transacted amid the most preternatural silence—was perpetrated so close to me that I was obliged to witness every revolting detail, and although I felt sure the victim was bad and vicious, I did not think the vileness of his character in any way justified the atrocity of his assassin.

"The murderer had barely accomplished his fiendish design before a deadly sickness came over me, and I fainted.

"On recovering consciousness, the room was once again in darkness, nor could I discover in the morning any sign whatever of the awful tragedy.

"On making inquiries in the town, I learned that the inn was well known to be haunted, other people, as well as I, having witnessed the same phenomenon, and that during the recent renovations a skeleton had been unearthed at the foot of the main staircase.

"I saw it in the local museum, and instantly identified the costume it wore as the one I had seen on the hapless fugitive. But—the skeleton was that of a WOMAN!"

NO. — SOUTHGATE STREET BRISTOL

THE NOTORIOUS SERVANT WHO ANSWERS THE DOOR

Technical form of apparition: Phantasm of the dead

Source of authenticity: (1) MS. signed by three eye-witnesses; (2) seen by author himself. Names of people and locality alone being altered

IN the spring of 1899, being then a member of a certain Psychical Research Society, and hearing that a ghost had been seen at No. — Southgate Street, Bristol, I set off to interview the ladies who were reported to have seen it. I found them (the Misses Rudd) at home, and on their very graciously consenting to relate to me their psychical experiences, I sat and listened to the following story (told as nearly as possible in the eldest lady's own words): "It is now," she began, "some ten years since we were the tenants of the house you mention, but I recollect what I saw there as vividly as if it were yesterday.

"The house, I must tell you, is very small (only eight or so rooms), dingy, and in a chronic state of dilapidation; it stands in the middle of a terrace with no front garden to speak of, save a few yards of moss-covered tiles, slate-coloured and broken, whilst its back windows overlooked a dreary expanse of deep and silent water. Nothing more dismal could be imagined.

"Still, when we took it, the idea of it being haunted never for one instant entered our minds, and our first intimation that such was the case came upon us like a thunderbolt.

"We only kept one maid, Jane (a girl with dark hair and pleasant manners), my sisters and I doing all the cooking and helping with the light work. The morning on which incident No. 1 happened, knowing Jane to be upstairs occupied in dusting the rooms, and my sisters being out, my mother asked me to go into the kitchen and see if the stove was all right as 'there was a smell of burning.'

"Doing as she bid, I hastened to the kitchen, where a strange spectacle met my sight.

"Kneeling in front of the stove, engaged apparently in polishing the fender, was a servant-girl with RED hair; I started back in astonishment. 'Who could she be?'

"Too intent at first to notice my advent, she kept on at her work, giving me time to observe that she was wearing a very dirty dress, and that her 'rag' of a cap was quite askew. Satisfied she was not 'Jane,' and wondering whether some one else's maid had mistaken our kitchen for her own—the houses in the terrace being all alike—I called out, 'Who are you? what do you want?'—whereupon, dropping the fire-irons with a clatter, she quickly turned round, displaying an ashen-pale face, the expression on which literally froze me with horror.

"Never! never had I seen such an awful look of hopeless, of desperate, of diabolical abandonment in any one's eyes as in those of hers when their glance met mine.

"For some seconds we glared at one another without moving, and then, still regarding me with a furtive look from out of the corner of her horrible eyes, she slowly rose from the hearth, and gliding stealthily forward, disappeared in the diminutive scullery opposite.

"Curiosity now overcoming fear, I at once followed. She was nowhere to be seen; nor was there any other mode of exit by which she could have made her departure than a tiny window, some four feet or so from the floor and directly overlooking the deep waters of the pond to which I have already alluded.

"Here, then, was a mystery! What had I seen? Had I actually encountered a phantasm, or was I but the victim of an exceedingly unpleasant and falsidical hallucination? I preferred to think the former.

"Not wishing to frighten my mother, I intended keeping the incident to myself, writing, however, a complete account of it in my diary for the current year, but, a further incident occurring to my youngest sister within the next few days, I determined to reveal what I had seen and compare notes."

The eldest Miss Rudd now concluded, and on my expressing a desire to hear more, her youngest sister very obligingly commenced:

"I had been out shopping in the Triangle one morning," she said, "and having omitted to take the latchkey, I was obliged to ring. Jane answered the summons. There was nothing, of course, unusual in this, as it was her duty to do so, but there was something extremely singular in what appeared at her elbow.

"Standing close beside—I might almost say, leaning against her (though Jane was apparently unaware of it)—was a strange, a VERY STRANGE, servant-girl, with RED HAIR and the most uncanny eyes; she had on a bedraggled print dress and a cap all askew; but it was her expression that most attracted my attention—it was HORRID.

"'Oh Jane!' I cried, 'whoever is it with you?'

"Following the direction of my gaze, Jane immediately turned round, and, without a word, FAINTED.

"That is all. The apparition, or whatever you may please to call it, vanished, and the next time I saw it was under different circumstances."

"Will you be so kind as to relate them?" I inquired.

Miss Rudd proceeded: "Oh! it is nothing very much!" she exclaimed, "only it was very unpleasant at the time—especially as I was all alone.

"You see, mother, being delicate, went to bed early, my sisters were at a concert, and it was Jane's 'night out.'

"I never, somehow, fancied the basement of the house; it was so cold and damp, reminding me not a little of a MORGUE or charnel-house; consequently I never stayed there a moment longer than was absolutely necessary, and on this night in question I was in the act of scurrying back to the drawing-room when a gentle tap! tap! at the scullery-window made me defer my departure. Entering the back kitchen, somewhat timidly I admit, I saw a face peering in at me through the tiny window.

"Though the night was dark and there was no artificial lighting at this side of the house, every feature of that face was revealed to me as clearly as if it had been day. The little, untidy cap, all awry, surmounting the shock-head of red hair now half-down and dripping with water, the ghastly white cheeks, the widely open mouth, and the eyes, their pupils abnormally dilated and full of lurid light, were more appallingly horrible than ever.

"I stood and gazed at it, my heart sick with terror, nor do I know what would have happened to me had not the loud rap of the postman acted like magic; the THING vanished, and 'turning tail,' I fled upstairs into the presence of my mother. That is all."

I was profuse in my thanks, and the third Miss Rudd then spoke:

"My bedroom," she began, "was on the top landing—the window over-looking the water. I slept alone some months after the anecdotes just related, and was awakened one night by feeling some disgusting, wet object lying on my forehead.

"With an ejaculation of alarm I attempted to brush it aside, and opening my eyes, encountered a ghastly white face bending right over me.

"I instantly recognised it, by the description my sisters had given, as the phantasm of the red-headed girl.

"The eyes were TERRIBLE! Shifting its slimy hand from my forehead, and brandishing it aloft like some murderous weapon, it was about to clutch my throat, when human nature would stand it no longer—and—I fainted. On recovering, I found both my sisters in the room, and after that I never slept by myself."

"Did your mother ever see it?" I asked.

"Frequently," the eldest Miss Rudd replied, "and it was chiefly on her account we relinquished our tenancy—her nervous system was completely prostrated."

"Other people saw the ghost besides us," the youngest Miss Rudd interrupted, "for not only did the long succession of maids after Jane ALL see it, but many of the subsequent tenants; the house was never let for any length of time."

"Then, perhaps, it is empty now?" I soliloquised, "in which case I shall most certainly experiment there."

This proved to be the case; the house was tenantless, and I easily prevailed upon the agent to loan me the key.

But the venture was fruitless. Three of us and a dog undertook it. We sat at the foot of the gloomy staircase; twelve o'clock struck, no ghost appeared, the dog became a nuisance—and—we came away disgusted.

A one-night's test, however, is no test at all; there is no reason to suppose apparitions are always to be seen by man; as yet we know absolutely nothing of the powers or conditions regulating their appearances, and it is surely feasible that the unknown controlling elements of one night may have been completely altered, may even have ceased to exist by the next. At all events, that was my opinion. I was by no means daunted at a single failure. But it was impossible to get any one to accompany me. The sceptic is so boastfully eager by day. "Ghosts," he sneers, "what are ghosts? Indigestion and imagination! I'll challenge you to show me the house I wouldn't sleep in alone! Ghosts indeed! Give me a poker or a shovel and I will scare away the lot of them." And when you do show him the house he always has a prior engagement, or else the weather is too cold, or he has too much work to do next day, or it isn't really worth the trouble, or—well! he is sure to have some very plausible excuse; at least, that has been my invariable experience.

There is no greater coward than the sceptic, and so, unable to procure a friend for the occasion, I did without one; neither did I have the key of the house, but—taking French leave—gained admittance through a window.

It was horribly dark and lonely, and although on the former occasion I did not feel the presence of the superphysical, I did so now, the very moment I crossed the threshold. Striking a light, I looked around me: I was in the damp and mouldy den that served as a kitchen; outside I saw the moon reflected on the black and silent water.

A long and sleek cockroach disappeared leisurely in a hole in the skirting as I flashed my light in its direction, and I thought I detected the movement of a rat or some large animal in the cupboard at the foot of the stairs. I forthwith commenced a search—the cupboard was empty. I must have been mistaken. For some minutes I stood in no little perplexity as to my next move. Where should I go? Where ought I to go if my adventure were to prove successful?

I glanced at the narrow, tortuous staircase winding upwards into the grim possibilities of the deserted hall and landings—and—my courage failed.

Here, at least, I was safe! Should the Unknown approach me, I could escape by the same window through which I had entered. I felt I dare not! I really COULD not go any further. Seized with a sudden panic at nothing more substantial than my own thoughts, I was groping my way backwards to the window when a revulsion of feeling made me pause. If all men were poltroons, how much would humanity ever know of the Occult? We should leave off where we began, and it had ever been my ambition to go—FURTHER.

My self-respect returning, I felt in my pocket for pencil, notebook and revolver, and trimming my lamp I mounted the stairs.

A house of such minute dimensions did not take long to explore; what rooms there were, were Lilliputian—mere boxes; the walls from which hung the tattered remnants of the most offensively inartistic papers were too obviously Jerry built; the wainscoting was scarred, the beading broken, not a door fitted, not a window that was not either loose or sashless—the entire house was rotten, paltry, mean; I would not have had it as a gift. But where could I wait to see the ghost?

Disgust at my surroundings had, for a time, made me forget my fears; these now returned reinforced: I thought of Miss Rudd's comparison with a morgue—and shuddered. The rooms looked ghastly! Selecting the landing at the foot of the upper storey, I sat down, my back against the wall—and—waited.

Confronting me was the staircase leading up and down, equally dark, equally ghostly; on my right was what might once have been the drawing-room, but was now a grim conglomeration of bare boards and moonlight, and on my left was an open window directly overtopping the broad expanse of colourless, motionless water. Twelve o'clock struck, the friendly footsteps of a pedestrian died away in the distance; I was now beyond the pale of assistance, alone and deserted—deserted by all save the slimy, creeping insects below—and the shadows. Yes! the shadows; and as I watched them sporting phantastically at my feet, I glanced into the darkness beyond—and shivered.

All was now intensely suggestive and still, the road alone attractive; and despite my spartonic resolutions I would have given much to be out in the open.

The landing was so cramped, so hopeless.

A fresh shadow, the shadow of a leaf that had hitherto escaped my notice, now attracted and appalled me; the scratching of an insect made my heart stand still; my sight and hearing were painfully acute; a familiar and sickly sensation gradually crept over me, the throbbing of my heart increased, the most inconceivable and desperate terror laid hold of me: the house was no longer empty—the supernatural had come! Something, I knew not, I dare not think what, was below, and I KNEW it would ascend.

All the ideas I had previously entertained of addressing the ghost and taking notes were entirely annihilated by my fear—fear mingled with a horrible wonder as to what form the apparition would take, and I found myself praying Heaven it might not be that of an ELEMENTAL.

The THING had now crossed the hall (I knew this somehow instinctively) and was beginning to mount the stairs.

I could not cry out, I could not stir, I could not close my eyes: I could only sit there staring at the staircase in the most awful of dumb, apprehensive agonies. The THING drew nearer, nearer; up, up, UP it came until I could see it at last—see the shock-head of red hair, the white cheeks, the pale, staring eyes, all rendered hideously ghastly by the halo of luminous light that played around it. This was a ghost—an apparition—a *bonâ fide* phantasm of the dead! And without any display of physical power—it overcame me.

Happily for me, the duration of its passage was brief.

It came within a yard of me, the water dripping from its clinging clothes, yet leaving no marks on the flooring. It thrust its face forward; I thought it was going to touch me, and tried to shrink away from it, but could not. Yet it did nothing but stare at me, and its eyes were all the more horrible because they were blank; not diabolical, as Miss Rudd had described them, but simply Blank!—Blank with the glassiness of the Dead.

Gliding past with a slightly swaying motion, it climbed upstairs, the night air blowing through the bedraggled dress in a horribly natural manner; I watched it till it was out of sight with bated breath—for a second or so it stopped irresolutely beside an open window; there was a slight movement as of some one mounting the sill: a mad, hilarious chuckle, a loud splash—and then—silence, after which I went home.

I subsequently discovered that early in the seventies a servant-girl, who was in service at that house, had committed suicide in the manner I have just described, but whether or not she had RED HAIR I have never been able to ascertain.

P.S.—The Ghost I am informed on very reliable authority, is still (August 1908) to be seen.

❑❑❑

MULREADY VILLA, NEAR BASINGSTOKE

THE BLACK CLOCK

Technical form of apparition: Either a phantasm of the dead or sub-human elemental

Source of authenticity: Eye-witness

Cause of haunting: A matter of surmise

WHEN I was reading for the Royal Irish Constabulary at that excellent and ever-popular Queen's Service Academy in Dublin, I made many friends among my fellow students, certain of whom it has been my good fortune to meet in after life.

Quite recently, for example, whilst on a visit of enjoyment to London, I ran up against T. at Daly's Theatre. T, one of the best-hearted fellows who ever trod in Ely Square, passed in second for the Royal Irish Constabulary, and is now a District Inspector in some outlandish village in Connemara.

And again, a summer or two ago, when I was on the pier at Bournemouth, I "plumped" myself down on a seat near to "G," who, although never a very great friend of mine, I was uncommonly glad to meet under the circumstances.

But last year I was unusually lucky, chancing to find, a passenger on the same boat as myself, Harry O'Moore, one of my very best "chums," from whom I learned the following story:

"You must know," he began, as we sat on deck watching the lofty outlines of St. David's Head slowly fade in the distance, "you must know, O'Donnell, that after leaving Crawley's I inherited a nice little sum of money from my aunt, Lady Maughan of Blackrock, who, dying quite unexpectedly, left the bulk of her property to my family. My brother Bob had her estate in Roscommon; Charley, the house near Dublin; whilst I—lucky beggar that I am—(for I was head over heels in debt at the time) suddenly found myself the happy possessor of £20,000 and—a bog-oak grandfather clock."

Here I thought fit to interrupt.

"A bog-oak clock!" I exclaimed. "Good gracious me! what a funny legacy! Had you taken a fancy to it?"

"I had never even seen it!" O'Moore laughed—then, looking suddenly serious: "My aunt, O'Donnell, as I daresay you recollect, was rather dry and satirical. The clock has not been exactly a pleasant acquisition to my establishment; so I fancy she may have bequeathed it to me as a sort of antidote to the exhilarating effect of £20,000. A sort of 'bitter with the sweet,' don't you know! You appear astonished! You would like to hear more about the clock? And you are quite right, too; the history of a really antique piece of furniture is a million times more interesting a subject to discuss than a ton of gold. To begin with, it was almost as new to my aunt as to me; she had only had it a week before she died, and during that brief interval she had made up her mind to leave it to me. Odd, was it not? I thought so, too, at her funeral! Now it seems quite natural; I was her metaphysician, I knew her and understood her idiosyncrasies better than most people. She bought the clock for a mere song from a second-hand furniture dealer in Grafton Street. I was living at the time near Basingstoke in a small house—one of those horrible anachronisms, an up-to-date villa in an old-world village.

"It's a charming neighbourhood—suited me down to the ground: flat country (hills tire me to death), excellent roads (I am fond of riding), trout streams, pretty meadows, crowds of honeysuckle and that sort of thing, and, to crown all else, Pines!!! Now, if there is one scent for which I have a special weakness, it is that of the pine. I could sit out of doors *ad infinitum* sniffing pines. It intoxicates me; hence I grew very fond of Hampshire.

"Let me return to the clock. It came from Dublin to Bristol *viâ* the good old Argo (what Bristolian is there, I should like to know, who doesn't love the Argo!) and thence by rail to Basingstoke, arriving at my house after dusk. You see, I am talking of it almost as if it were some live person! But then, you see, it was a bog-oak grandfather's clock—no common grinder I can assure you; and I was prepared to pay it every homage the moment it was landed in the hall.

"The carter, however, was by no means so enamoured of it; he was a rough, churlish fellow (what British workmen is not?). 'If you take my advice, mister!' he growled, 'you'll pitch the himpish thing in some one helse's garden rightaway.' (How characteristic of the charitable Briton.)

"I gently rebuked the irate man. Of course, he could afford to be more prodigal with his belongings than I. With evident haste, and still muttering angrily, he went—and I—I called to my housekeeper (Mrs. Partridge), and we examined the heirloom together.

"It certainly was a most imposing piece of furniture. Standing at least eight feet high, with a face large in proportion, it towered above me like a giant negro—black—I can't describe to you how black—black as ebony and shining.

"I asked Mrs. Partridge how she liked it; for, to tell you the truth, there was something so indefinably queer about it that I began to wonder if the carter had spoken the truth.

"'It is truly magnificent!' she said, running her hand over its polished surface, 'I have never seen so fine a piece of workmanship! It will be the making of this hall—but—it reminds me of a hearse!!!'

"We laughed—the analogy was simply ludicrous. A grandfather's clock and a hearse! But then—it told the Time! and Time is sometimes represented in the guise of Death! Father Death with the sickle!

"My laughter left me and I shivered.

"We placed the clock in the right-hand corner of the hall, opposite the front door, so that every one coming to the house could see it; and, as we anticipated, it was much admired—so much admired, in fact, that I became quite jealous—jealous, and of a clock! How very singular. But then I recollected I was 'engaged,' and, of course, I resented my *fiancée* taking notice of any one or anything save myself.

"Like all the other visitors, however, she never passed by the clock without pausing to look at it.

"'I can't help it,' she whispered. 'It's its size! it's stupendous! It quite fills the house! there is hardly any room to breathe! It's a monstrous clock! It fascinates me! It's more than a clock. You must GET RID of it.'

"Avice was whimsical. What, get rid of the Ebony Clock! Impossible—the idea tickled me. I laughed.

"I laughed then—but not later, when she had gone and all was quiet.

"From the hall below I heard it strike one, two, three—twelve!

"Its pendulum swung to and fro with a dull and ponderous clang, and the sound that came from its brazen lungs, though loud and deep and musical, was far too thrilling.

"Against my will, it made me think, and my thoughts were none too pleasant.

"Hardly had its vibrations ceased before I sat up in bed and listened! At first I attributed the noise I had heard to the pulsations of my heart—bump! bump! bump!—but as I crouched there, waiting, I was soon undeceived; the sounds not only increased in intensity, but drew nearer—bump! bump! bump!—just as if something huge and massive was moving across the hall floor and ascending the stairs!

"An icy fear stole all over me! What!—what in Heaven's name could it be?

"I glanced in terror at the door—it was locked—locked and BOLTED—the village was much frequented by tramps, and I always went to bed prepared.

"But this noise—this series of heavy, mechanical booms—THIS could never be attributed to any burglar!

"It reached the top of the staircase, it pounded down the passage leading to my room; and then, with the most terrific crash, it FELL against my door!

"I was spellbound—petrified. I dared not—I COULD NOT move.

"It was the clock! the gigantic, monstrous clock!—the funereal, hideous clock! I heard it ticking! The suspicions that I entertained all along with regard to it were now confirmed—it lived!!! That was no ordinary striking—THIS was no ordinary ticking. The thing breathed, it spoke, it laughed—laughed in some diabolically ghoulish manner.

"I would have sacrificed my house and fortune to have been able to reach the bell. I could not. I could do nothing but sit there listening—listening to its mocking voice. The minutes passed by slowly—never had I had the leisure to count them with such painful accuracy; for the tickings, though of equal duration, varied most alarmingly in intonation.

"This horrible farce lasted without cessation till one, when, apparently convinced of its inability to gain admittance, it gave an extra loud and emphatic clang and took its departure.

"In the morning it was standing as usual in its corner in the hall, nor could I detect the slightest evidences of animation, neither in its glassy face nor in its sepulchral tone.

"Happening to pass by at that instant, Mrs. Partridge surprised me in my act of examination, and from her ashy cheeks and frightened glances I concluded she, too, had heard the noises and had rightly guessed their origin. Nor was I mistaken, for, on putting a few leading questions to her, she reluctantly admitted she had heard everything. 'But,' she whispered, 'I have kept it from the maids, for if once they get hold of the idea the house is haunted they will leave to-morrow.'

"Unfortunately, her circumspection proved of no avail; night after night the clock repeated its vagaries, bumping on the staircases and passages to such a degree that the noise not only awakened the entire household, but aroused general suspicion.

"Nor were its attentions any longer restricted to me; it gradually extended the length of its wanderings till every part of the house had been explored and every door visited.

"The maids now complained to me. 'They could not do their work,' they argued, 'if they were deprived of sleep, and sleep was out of the question whilst the disturbances continued. I must get rid of the clock.'

"To this proposition, however, I was by no means agreeable. I certainly had no reason to like the clock—indeed I loathed and hated it—but in some indefinable manner it fascinated me. I could not, I dare not part with it. 'I have no doubt,' I protested, 'the annoyances will cease as soon as the clock has become at home with its surroundings. Have patience and all will be well.'

"They agreed to wait a little longer before giving me notice, and I fully hoped that my prophecy would be fulfilled. But the clock was far more persistent than I had anticipated. Adopting fresh tactics, it began a series of persecutions that speedily brought matters to a crisis.

"Christina, the cook, was the first victim.

"Not being a very fluent scribe, her letters caused her endless labour, and she often sat up writing long after the other servants had gone to bed.

"On the night in question she was plodding on wearily when the intense stillness of the house made her suddenly think of the time; it must be very late! Dare she venture in the hall?

"Christina was not a nervous woman; she had hitherto discredited all ghost-stories, and was quite the last person in the house to accept the theory that the present disturbances were due to any superphysical agency. She now, however, recollected all that had been said on the subject, and the close proximity of the clock filled her with dread; her fears being further augmented by the knowledge of her isolation—unluckily her room was completely cut off from any other in the house.

"Hastily putting away her writing materials, she was preparing to make a precipitate rush for the stairs when a peculiar thumping riveted her attention.

"Her blood congealed, her legs tottered, she could not move an inch. What was it?

"Her heart—only the pulsations of her heart.

"She burst out laughing. How truly ridiculous.

"Catching her breath and casting fearful looks of apprehension on all sides, she advanced towards the stairs and 'tiptoeing' stealthily across the hall, tried in vain to keep her eyes from the clock. But its sonorous ticking brought her to a peremptory halt.

"She stood and listened. Tick! tick! tick! It was so unlike any other ticking she had ever heard, it appalled her.

"The clock, too, seemed to have become blacker and even more gigantic.

"It reared itself above her like a monstrous coffin.

"She was now too terrified to think of escape, and could only clutch hold of the bannisters in momentary terror of some fresh phenomenon.

"In this helpless condition she watched the clock slowly increase in stature till its grotesquely carved summit all but swept the ceiling, whilst a pair of huge, toeless, grey feet protruded from beneath its base.

"Nor were these the only changes, for during their accomplishment others of an equally alarming nature had taken place, and the ticking, after having passed through many transitional stages, was now replaced by a spasmodic breathing, forcibly suggestive of something devilish and bestial.

"At this juncture words cannot convey any idea of what Christina suffered; nor had she seen the worst.

"Midnight at length came. In dumb agony she watched the minute-hand slowly make its last circuit; there were twelve frantic clangs, the door concealing the pendulum flew open, and an enormous hand, ashy grey, with long, mal-shaped fingers, made a convulsive grab at her.[1] Swinging to one side, she narrowly avoided capture and, glancing upwards, saw something so diabolically awful that her heart turned to ice.

"The face of the clock had disappeared, and in its place Christina saw a frightful head—grey and evil. It was very large and round, half human, half animal, and wholly beastly, with abnormally long, lidless eyes of pale blue that leered at the affrighted girl in the most sinister manner.

"Such a creature must have owed its origin to Hell.

"For some seconds she stared at it, too enthralled with horror even to breathe; and, then a sudden movement on its part breaking the spell, she regained control over her limbs and fled for her life.

• • • •

"CHRISTINA REPORTED all this to me the next morning. She had narrowly escaped capture by darting through the front door which some one, fortunately for her, had forgotten to bolt. She had not returned to the house, but had, instead, passed the rest of the night in a neighbouring cottage.

"'I won't, under any circumstances, sir,' she added, 'sleep here again. Indeed, I could not, because I can't abide the presence of that clock. I shan't feel easy until I am miles away from it—in some big town, where the bustle and noise of life may help me to forget it—FORGET it!!'—and she shuddered.

"Partly as a compensation for what she had undergone and partly to avoid a scandal, I presented her with a substantial cheque.

"Despite Mrs. Partridge's pleadings, I kept the clock. I could not—I dare not—part with it. It was my aunt's bequest—it fascinated me! Do you understand, O'Donnell?—it fascinated me.

"But I did make one concession: I permitted them to remove it to the summer-house.

"My first care now was to see that all the doors were locked, and windows bolted before retiring to bed; a precaution that was speedily justified.

"For the next few nights after the removal of the clock I was awakened about twelve by a violent ringing of the front door bell, whilst a heavy crunching of the gravel beneath my window informed me our persecutor was trying to gain admittance.

"These nocturnal disturbances ceasing, I had begun to congratulate myself upon having seen the last of the hauntings, when a rumour reached me that the clock had actually begun to infest the more lonely of the lanes and by-roads.

"Nor did this report, as the sequel will show, long remain unverified.

"My uncle John, a rare old 'sport,' came to stay with me. He arrived about ten, and we had not yet gone to bed when the vicar of the parish burst into our presence in the greatest state of agitation.

"'I must apologise for this late visit,' he gasped, sinking into an easy chair, 'I couldn't get here before. Indeed, I did not intend calling this evening, and would not have done so but for an extraordinary incident that has just happened. Would you think it very unclerical if I were to ask you for a glass of neat brandy?'

"I glanced at him in ill-disguised terror. His blanched cheeks and trembling hands told their own tale—he had seen the clock.

"'Thanks awfully,' he said, replacing the empty glass on the table. 'I feel better now—but, by jove! it DID unnerve me. Let me tell you from the beginning. I had been calling at Gillet's Farm, which, as you know, is two or more miles from here, and the night being fine, I decided to go home by the fields. Well! all was right till I got to the little spinney lying at the foot of Dickson's Hollow.

"'Even in broad daylight I always feel a trifle apprehensive before entering it, as it is often frequented by tramps and other doubtful characters: in fact, there isn't a more murderous looking spot in the county.

"'All was so still, so unusually still I thought, and the shadows so incomprehensible that I had half a mind to retrace my steps, but, disliking to appear cowardly, and remembering, I must confess, that I had ordered a roast duck for supper, I climbed the wooden fence and plunged into the copse.

"'At every step the silence increased, the cracking of twigs under my feet sounding like the report of firearms, whilst it grew so dark that I had in certain places literally to feel my way. When about halfway through the wood the shrubs that line the path on either side abruptly terminate, bringing into view a circle of sward, partially covered with ferns and bracken, and having in its midst a stunted willow that has always struck me as being peculiarly out of place there.

"'Indeed, I was pondering over this incongruity when a tall figure stalked out from behind the tree, and, gliding swiftly forward, took to the path ahead of me.

"'I rubbed my eyes and stared in amazement, and no doubt you will think me mad when I tell you the figure was nothing human.'

"'What was it, then—an anthropoid ape?' my Uncle John laughed.

"The vicar shook his head solemnly.

"'I will describe it to you to the best of my ability,' he said. 'To begin with it was naked—stark, staring naked!'

"'How positively indecent,' murmured Uncle John, 'really vicar, I don't wonder you were frightened.'

"'And then,' the vicar continued, disregarding the interruption, 'it was grey!—from head to foot a uniform livid grey.'

"'A grey monstrosity! Ah! now THAT is interesting!'

"I looked at my uncle quizzically—was he still joking? But no! he was in sober earnest: could it be possible he knew anything about the clock.

"I leaned back in my chair and smiled—feebly.

"'In height,' the vicar went on, 'it could not have been far from seven feet, it had an enormous round head crowned with a black mass of shock hair, no ears, huge spider-like hands and toeless feet.

"'I could not see its face as its back was turned on me.

"'Urged on by an irresistible impulse (although half dead with terror), I followed the Thing.

"'Striding noiselessly along, it left the spinney, and crossing several fields entered your grounds by the gate in the rear of the house.'

"'What!' my uncle roared, banging the table with his fist, 'what! do you mean to tell me you allowed it to come here!'

"'I couldn't stop it,' the vicar said apologetically, stretching forward to help himself to some more brandy. 'It led me to your summer-house, vanishing through the doorway. Resolved on seeing the last, and hoping thereby to discover some clue to the mystery, I cautiously approached the window, and, peering through the glass, saw the creature walk stealthily across the floor and disappear into a gigantic clock. I verily believe I was as much scared by the sight of that clock as I had been by the appearance of the spectre—they were both satanically awful.'

"'Is that all?' my Uncle John inquired.

"'It is,' the vicar replied, 'and is it not enough?'

"My Uncle John got on his feet.

"'Before returning a verdict,' he said, 'I must see the clock. Let us go to the summer-house at once.'

"The vicar and I were loud in our protests—'We were sure my uncle must be tired; better put off the investigation to the morrow.'

"It was, however, of no avail; there was no gainsaying Uncle John when once he had made up his mind to do anything.

"We accordingly escorted him without further delay to the garden.

"The clock was standing quite peacefully where I had had it set.

"As soon as my uncle saw it he caught hold of my arm. 'Where on earth did you get it from, Harry?' he cried, bubbling over with excitement. 'The last time I saw that clock was in Kleogh Castle, the home of the Blakes. It had been in their possession for centuries, and was made from what is supposed to be the oldest bog-oak in Ireland. Ah! the old lady left it you, did she? and you say she got it from Kelly's in Grafton Street.

"'Come! that explains everything. The Blakes—poor beggars—were sold up last year, and Kelly's, I know, were represented at the sale.

"'But now comes the extraordinary part of the affair. The grey figure our friend the vicar has just described to us tallies exactly with the phantasm that used to haunt Kleogh, and which the Blakes have always regarded in the light of a family ghost.

"'Now it would appear that they are entirely wrong—that it is with the clock and not Kleogh this apparition is connected—a fact that is not at all surprising when we come to consider its origin and the vast antiquity of its frame.

"'But let us examine it more carefully to-morrow.'

"We did so, and discovered that the frontal pillars on either side of the face of the clock consisted of two highly polished femur-bones which, although blackened through countless ages of immersion in the bog, and abnormally long (as is inevitably the case with Paleolithic man), were very unmistakably human.

• • • •

"I RETURNED THE CLOCK anonymously to Kelly's."[2]

□□□

NO. — PARK STREET, BATH

THE HORRIBLE COUGHING ON THE STAIRS

Technical form of apparition: Phantasm of the dead
Cause of haunting: Murder
Source of authenticity: Reliable hearsay evidence

BATH is a veritable cockpit of Ghostdom; its grey and venerable mansions abound in ghosts; it is for its size the most psychic town in England.

I say this because I have at my elbow no less than twenty-five well authenticated stories of haunted houses in this city: a collection that is numerically superior to that of any other town in England, saving London, and to the ghosts of London there is, as I stated at my recent lecture in Chandos Street, no end—positively no end.

One evening last January I read a paper on "My Superphysical Experiences" before an extremely intelligent, and, I venture to say, appreciative audience of Theosophists, at their headquarters, Argyll Street, Bath.

Among the number was a gentleman—quite a stranger I believe—who gave me his card and asked me to call on him next day. I did so, and in the course of a very entertaining chat he narrated to me the following story:

"Some years ago some friends of mine, named Hartley, took a house in Park Street, which, as you may know, is built on the side of a hill.

"The house suited them; it was warm, dry, and in a very tolerable state of repair; it was also in a quiet and thoroughly respectable part of the town, and the rent was low—ridiculously low—so low, indeed, that they began to wonder why it was so low.

"Anxious to find out if their neighbours were equally fortunate in the matter of rent, they made enquiries, and learned to their astonishment that every other house in the row was let at more than double the price of theirs.

"Why was this? Was their landlord a philanthropist, a Carnegie, a madman, or what?

"Or did the house contain some subtle flaw they were yet to discover to their disadvantage? Perhaps, very much to their disadvantage; for they were sufficiently worldly to discredit sentiment in business!

"Getting on the track of former tenants, they plied them with cautious questions; it was of no avail, the bait did not take; they could ascertain nothing. Then they gave up—and the truth at last leaked out.

"One dreary afternoon in a particularly dreary November, I believe it was the fourth of November, the Rev. Silas Wetherby, vicar of an adjoining Parish, called on them.

"They were delighted to see him; Mrs. Hartley was fond of the clergy; her father and uncles and brothers were all in the Church; she had lived in a clerical atmosphere from the day she was born.

"But the Rev. Silas Wetherby puzzled her. Had he been a deacon, a *locum*, or a newly ordained curate, she would have passed him over as excusably shy; but he was too old a stager for that. Why did he puzzle her, then? He was orthodox, urbane, and—she would stake her handkerchief—no small tatler of ecclesiastical gossip, but yet there was something amiss with him, something that made him pause, something that made him fidget.

"Probably she never would have found out why he behaved in such an odd manner but for an unexpected occurrence.

"Without even as much as a rap, Bobby, their youngest boy, who is, as a rule, very shy before visitors, suddenly burst into the room. He was pale with excitement.

"'Oh, do come, mummy,' he cried, 'there is such a queer old man in such a quaint dress on the staircase. He is coughing horribly. I fancy he must be very sick. Do come, mummy—please.'

"Mr. Wetherby's behaviour was now odd in the extreme. Half rising from his seat and trembling all over, he pointed his finger violently at the door.

"'Run away, little man,' he said, 'run away! No one is coughing now. Your invalid has recovered, he is gone. Go directly, and shut the door behind you. Mind—shut the door, and keep clear of the staircase,' and Bobby, completely at a loss what to make of this despotic stranger, beat a hasty retreat.

"Mrs. Hartley, disregarding the pleading look from her husband, was about to expostulate; like the majority of modern mothers, her tender—might I add unsound—sensibilities could not bear to see her offspring treated in any but the most deferential manner.

"The Rev. Silas, however, forestalled her. With a wave of his hand that was as eloquent as it was peremptory he completely took the wind out of her sails, and before she had time to recover from her surprise he had commenced:

"'For Heaven's sake, Mrs. Hartley!' he said in a semi-whisper, leaning forward in such a manner as emphasised the mysterious air he had suddenly assumed, 'for Heaven's sake! leave this house as quickly as you can!'

"'There now, Arthur!' Mrs. Hartley exclaimed, the angry expression in her eyes being replaced by a mixture of triumph and curiosity—'There now! didn't I tell you all along something was wrong with the place?'

"'Drains, I suppose!' her husband said mournfully, 'drains or rats!—and I do hate moving.'

"'Neither one nor the other!' the Rev. Silas whispered. 'No! the house is haunted.'

"At this announcement Mrs. Hartley gave a slight ejaculation of terror—an ejaculation which, reduced to its constituent parts, might be found to consist of affectation, fear, and no small amount of pleasure, the latter engendered by the glamour of something both ENIGMATICAL and FASHIONABLE.

"'What's it haunted by? Teapots?' Mr. Hartley muttered with a contemptuous movement of his mouth. 'If it's not haunted by teapots now, it will be some day, for that new maid of yours, my dear, is always breaking them. She has smashed two since yesterday, and if you examine this one closely you will observe that the spout is already chipped.'

"Mrs. Hartley puckered her dainty brows into the most alarming frown.

"'Really, Arthur! how mundane you are,' she remarked loftily; then, turning to Mr. Wetherby, 'My husband is, as you see, one of those solid individuals who believes in nothing till he sees it.'

"'And not always then,' Arthur murmured, gazing intently at the parson as the latter was about to pour the contents of the cream-jug into his cup. 'Everything that appears to the eye white and sticky is not cream! Some animals have brains, even pigs—and some dairymen are frauds—most of them!'

"'Good gracious me!' the Rev. Silas cried hastily replacing the jug. 'You surely don't mean to insinuate——'

"'He doesn't mean anything!' Mrs. Hartley interrupted with considerable impatience, 'he is unusually silly this afternoon—so pray excuse him!' and—with the regular six-months-in-Paris accent—'revenons à nos moutons, s'il vous plait. I am anxious to hear about the ghost.'

"Mr. Wetherby looked a trifle sulky; he fought shy of sceptics, and he no longer enjoyed his tea.

"'Now, mind I don't ask you to believe me!' he began, 'although there are plenty of people in this parish who will confirm what I say; but eighty, or a hundred or so years ago, a son poisoned his father in this very house.

"'The manner of the poisoning was quite orthodox—arsenic in apple dumplings. There have been many parallel cases, chiefly, I believe, in Liverpool.

"'Arsenic being an irritant, causes considerable vomiting, hence the old man must have had several attacks of sickness prior to the one that terminated his existence as he was travelling downstairs to fetch a doctor. He died, it is said, in excruciating agony on the landing at the top of the first flight of stairs.'

"'And it is his ghost that haunts the house?' Mrs. Hartley hazarded.

"The Rev. gentleman nodded. 'Just so,' he said, 'and it was this apparition, undoubtedly, that your little boy saw just now. It always appears on November 4, the anniversary of the murder, and—' Mr. Wetherby was going to add something that, judging from the increased solemnity of his voice, would have been very impressive, when Mr. Hartley cut in: 'Then at all events we shall have a reprieve, a year's undisputed possession, subject to no interference on the part of the spook—Mr. Whatever's his name.' He laughed irreverently, 'You certainly won't catch me giving up this lease for any so immaterial a reason. No, thank you! I cannot get as good a bargain as this every day in the week!'

"The Rev. Silas rose to go. 'Very well then!' he said, bowing stiffly, 'I could say more—but I won't! I am sorry I have said as much. Some sceptics are never convinced! Some sceptics do not wish to be convinced! Some sceptics may be convinced, but prefer to appear unconvinced!

"'I am no metaphysician! I will not attempt to classify YOU. I will only say, "May you never be AFRAID."

"'I trust Mrs. Hartley, at all events, is not a sceptic: I hope she is not a psychic! especially not a psychic in this house. I wish you good day!'

"'He did not wish us good luck!' Mr. Hartley explained as the door banged. 'By Jove! I have no patience to listen to such stuff! Haunted, indeed!'

"But his wife shook her head. 'Scepticism is one thing, and what Bobbie saw is another!' she argued. 'You can't get over that, Arthur! Now, are we doing the right thing for the children in remaining here?'

"In all matters concerning her children Mrs. Hartley's instincts were always acute—one or two of them were babies, even younger than Bobbie.

"On this occasion, however, Mr. Hartley held his own. 'BOBBIE,' he reasoned, 'must have had the daymare, and even if he did see anything, no harm has come of it. You must recollect, my dear,' he observed, 'that I have not been doing over-well on the Stock Exchange lately; moving is a costly thing, and if I spend money in one way, I must recoup in another, which means no new dress for you and no Weston-super-Mare for the children.'

"The validity of this logic was not lost upon Mrs. Hartley. She reflected; and then with her customary adroitness gave a turn to the conversation.

• • • •

"IT WAS ONCE AGAIN NOVEMBER, the fourth of November, and the staircase incident of a year ago now seemed remote and improbable. It was, however, uppermost in the minds of both Mr. and Mrs. Hartley, though they both pretended to have forgotten it.

"They had neither seen Mr. Wetherby again, nor had they mentioned the appearance of the ghost to anyone. It was really of so little consequence.

"It was a wet afternoon—wet and chilly, and as neither Mr. or Mrs. Hartley had any particular inducement to face the elements, they decided to stay indoors, Mrs. Hartley reclining in an easy chair before the drawing-room fire whilst her husband seated himself in like manner before a blazing hearth in the dining-room.

"They tried to read—they could not; they tried to sleep—they could not: and somehow they felt that they ought to go and look at the children—but they would not; and so they whiled away the hours in this half-hearted and wholly unsatisfactory manner.

"It seems the sudden opening of the nursery door first disturbed Mrs. Hartley, and fancying she heard someone steal gently across the landing, she called out; there was no reply, so, thinking it was fancy, she was about to settle down again when the sound of some one coughing made her heart beat quickly.

"Who could it be? Not the nurse! The nurse wouldn't cough in such a deep and hoarse manner! nor yet Arthur; she would recognise his cough anywhere. Hark! there it was again—cough! cough! cough! just as if some one was being sick. Someone being sick! Ah! who could that someone be? who indeed? but—and fearing lest one of the children might be on the stairs, she overcame a momentary weakness and sallied forth.

"What she saw froze her with horror.

"At the top of the hall staircase was the figure of a man clad in the costume of the eighteenth century, viz., long maroon tail-coat with vest to match, knee breeches, and coarse yellow stockings. Mrs. Hartley couldn't see his face, as he was in a recumbent position and vomiting horribly. Looking up at him from below, her eyes big with pity and wonder—not fear—was Kitty, the Hartley's youngest child.

"Catching sight of her mother, Kitty cried, 'Oh! mummy, do tum down! the poor man is awful ill. Do help him! I'll tum too,' and suiting the action to her words the little mite prepared to ascend. No sooner, however, had she set a foot on the staircase than the old man slipped, and, falling sideways, plunged through the air.

"Making sure Kitty would be hurt, and regardless of the fact that she was merely clutching at a phantom, Mrs. Hartley appears to have made frantic efforts to stay the disaster. Whether in her agitation she tried to go down the stairs too quickly, or whether in her anxiety to save her child she lost her head and simply leaped forward, it is impossible to say; she herself always declares that the stairs 'collapsed' under her.

Anyhow, she fell, and crashing into Kitty, literally crushed the life out of her. Mr. Hartley found mother and child lying together at the foot of the stairs, and although he saw no sign of any apparition, he is no longer a sceptic.

"His wife recovered—at least, she is alive—though I am told some internal complaint—the result of the catastrophe—makes her long for death.

"Some months after Kitty's burial, when time had to a certain extent mollified the poignancy of suffering caused by her death, Mr. Hartley received a letter of condolence from the Rev. Silas Wetherby.

"The greater portion of the epistle was simply a formal declaration of sympathy, but the concluding lines, inasmuch as they bear on the haunting, are worth repeating.

"The worthy divine wrote as follows:

"'If you recollect, at our last meeting I gave you to understand that I had something further to tell you *re* the occult disturbances in your late abode.

"'You will probably treat my statement with contempt, badly concealed under cover of a pretty pasquinade, but I am prepared to run the gauntlet of your scepticism in order to relieve my conscience.

"'What I would have told you had I not been silenced (culpably I own) by your ridicule, is this: the appearance of the sick man had always been followed by some dire calamity, whenever any attempt has been made to set even as much as one foot on the staircase during the manifestations—hence my warning to Bobbie.

"'I cannot, of course, explain to you why a phenomenon of this sort should entail physical disaster any more than I can elucidate the mystery of the Ghost Candles of Wales, or the Banshees of Ireland, between which manifestations and the phenomena in question there is a strong analogy. But should you feel sufficiently interested in the subject to ask for further information, or even be sufficiently dubious to demand testimony, I will with pleasure provide you with an abundance of creditable corroborations both documentary and oral.'

"But Mr. Hartley was perfectly satisfied."

❑❑❑

THE MINERY, DEVON

THE MAN WITH THE BUCKET

Technical form of apparition: Phantasm of dead

Source of authenticity: Letter from the person who saw the ghost

Cause of haunting: Murder

HOTEL RIETZ, VIENNA.

Feb. 10, 1908.

DEAR MR. O'DONNELL,

In reply to your inquiry as to that psychic experience I had in Devon, I will do my best to make the affair explicit, although, as you know very well, I do not pose as a scribe.

Well! it took place three years ago—June 15th, 1905—shall I ever forget the date! My friends, the Maitlands had only just taken "The Minery," a pretty yellow stone villa, modern in every respect. It stood some few yards away from the road and was fronted by a lawn, bordered with honeysuckle, sweet-peas and Devon roses.

I tell you this to impress upon you the fact that there was positively nothing suggestive of ghosts either in the grounds or building, the latter being as unlike the orthodox haunted house as one can well imagine. If anything should have warned me it was the hesitating and half nervous manner (so unlike herself) with which Dora Maitland showed me my room.

"I do hope you will like it and be comfortable, dear!" she said as she stood for a moment on the threshold, a strangely perplexing expression in her eyes, and one which I couldn't then interpret. "Be sure to tell us if you DON'T and we will have you moved at once."

"Why shouldn't I?" I asked in unfeigned astonishment. "It is delightfully snug and sunny—a south aspect—a charming view and—oh! the most delightful of dainty furniture. Why, Dora! I should indeed be an ungrateful Sybarite if I didn't revel in it." And Dora forced a smile.

The hot summer days drove us into the open: we got up early and went to bed late. Being a man, and fond of cricket and fishing, you would hardly appreciate the life we led. We are women of the old school, and consequently spent all our time at home on the lawn, plying our needles, possibly at the same time chewing chocolates or discussing our favourite books; motoring and golf we left to others.

The 15th of June was warm and sultry; we had been invited to spend the evening at the adjoining vicarage; Dora had a headache, her mother was a chronic invalid, and so—willy-nilly—I went alone.

It was a stupid affair: mediocre music, still more mediocre supper—and—BRIDGE!

Fancy Bridge in a sleepy country Parsonage, fancy Bridge anywhere! I hate Bridge!

The guests were of the usual sort, prudish, prosy and plain; a widow and twins, the Miss Somebodies of Somewhere; a curate, a doctor and a lawyer! What (with the exception of the last) could be more respectable, what more dull—deadly dull?

They were all (the men, I mean) very anxious I should play cards, but for once in a way I made myself positively disagreeable—and sat—alone!

Eleven o'clock came. It was time to go! I rose with alacrity, omitting, I believe, in the intensity of joy, the formal expressions of regret.

The vicar accompanied me as far as the gates; bidding me a bland good-night, he retraced his steps with a sigh of relief. Mrs. Maitland had left a light burning in the hall. I turned it out, and taking up my candle proceeded to my bedroom and was beginning to undress when a strange thing happened.

My bedroom door (which I felt positively certain I had locked) slowly opened and a man peered in.

I can see him now—strong, regular features with piercing dark and somewhat sinister eyes that were in marked contrast to the iron-grey brows and wavy, neatly parted hair. The chin was square, the head well shaped; he was a handsome man, yet he did not please me!

I was frightened.

For some seconds he glanced furtively round the room, his eyes finally resting on the bedstead, which he regarded in a manner that made my flesh creep! Who could he be? what on earth did he want?

Terrified lest he should see me—though why it was he hadn't done so I couldn't for the life of me imagine—I kept shrinking backwards, backwards into the alcove where I hung my dresses, in the wild hope that they would afford me a safe hiding-place.

Presently, to my unutterable relief, he disappeared, and I heard his footsteps tiptoeing gently down the staircase.

Here then was my chance of escape! Hardly daring to breathe, I rushed frantically to the door (Heaven preserve me!—it was locked again!) and tearing it open, I made directly for the passage leading to Dora's room.

On my way I heard a noise—a noise that fascinated and kept me still—the clanging of a bucket.

What could a man be doing with a bucket at this time of night—a bucket!—and on that staircase so daintily furnished with velvet pile?

Breathlessly I watched him ascend, his step light and springing, his head bent low, and the bucket clanging each time he mounted—clang! clang! clang!

The agony I suffered—for I could now only conclude he was either a madman or burglar—was indescribable; I dreaded above all things the act of being seen—of encountering a glance from those evil eyes.

Nearer and nearer he came! One more step, and he stood on the little lobby outside my bedroom door. What was he going to do—to enter my room or follow me?

My heart stood still; a cold sweat burst out all over me; I essayed to shriek and implore the aid of Dora; my throat dried up, my tongue stuck to the palate of my mouth—I was speechless! helpless! hopeless! Another yard, and the uncanny stranger would have me in his clutches.

At the crucial moment Heaven heard my silent prayer; he halted, I was saved! With one hand on the handle, he slowly—very slowly—opened the door, and crouching down on his hands and feet, crept quietly in, muffling the sound of the bucket.

Incongruous sight!—a man, a madman, or a burglar with a common, an every-day bucket, and in the ecstasies of salvation I gave a weak, hysterical laugh!—a madman with a bucket! and what a bucket!

After this little display of emotion, and being now in the full possession of all my motive faculties, I promptly fled, not pausing for the fraction of a second till I had reached the bedside of Dora and had shaken her to wakefulness. She listened to my story with blanched cheeks, beseeching me with terror in her eyes to make sure the door was locked and that her Bible was well in evidence.

Her fears adding to my own, for I now concluded that there was some horrible mystery attached to what I had just witnessed, I hastily scrambled into bed, and, drawing the clothes well over our heads, begged her to confide in me the secret.

"I hardly know how to explain it, Kate," she whispered, "you will be so shocked! and I'm afraid you will blame us horribly for putting you in that room; but, to tell you the truth, we had nowhere else—at least nowhere suitable, as the ceilings and walls are sadly out of repair.

"You see, we bought this house at a very low price; it had stood empty for a good many months, was in a sad state of dilapidation, and the owner was only too glad to get rid of it.

"After we had settled in, he coolly informed us that it was reputed to be haunted; that the remains of a woman had been found under the cement of the back-kitchen floor (it is now nicely tiled), and that on the anniversary of its committal the tragedy was reported to be re-enacted in all its grim details."

"And was she murdered in my room?" I inquired.

"It is supposed so," Dora murmured. "There is a tell-tale stain (which nothing will efface) under the carpet—and—former tenants are reported to have seen all you have witnessed, and rather more."

"And the murderer! what of him?" I asked, thinking with a shudder of his eyes.

"No one knows anything!" Dora whispered, edging closer to me as we heard a distant clang. "It is only surmised he was her husband—she was quite a stranger here—and—he was never caught."

"But the bucket, what could he want with such an absurd thing as a bucket?" and as I heard it clanging from below I gave a ghastly chuckle.

"For Heaven's sake don't laugh!" Dora shivered. "They found that bucket—he had used it for transporting her remains!"

• • • •

Please remember me, &c., to all.
Ever yours sincerely,
KATHLEEN M. DEAN.

❑❑❑

THURLOW HALL,[3] NEAR EXETER

FIRE! FIRE! BRING ME FIRE!

Technical form of apparition: Phantasm of dead
Source of authenticity: First-hand evidence

THE following story was related to me by Miss Constance Delaunay, and is given as near as possible in her own words:

"The early spring of 1898 was, I daresay you remember, exceptionally fine—so fine, indeed, that my mother, a chronic sufferer from rheumatism, determined to remain in England instead of going, as was her custom, to the Riviera.

"We did not want, however, to stay in town, an unusually gay Christmas having given us an appetite for the country; so we sub-let our flat and took Thurlow Hall, furnished, on a three months' lease.

"We had never been to Devon; we had heard much of its beauty; we were disappointed.

"Possibly, being of foreign extraction, I am prejudiced, but in my opinion the scenery of Devon is almost, if not quite, as inferior to that of Belgium and Switzerland as the manners of its peasants are inferior to those of the corresponding class of Continentals.

"The West Country rustics did not impress us favourably; on our arrival they welcomed us with gapes and stares and boorish grunts; not a few of them giggled, whilst others, slouching up to our boxes, read the labels and muttered disparaging things about foreigners.

"We were told it was the spirit of independence, a spirit presumably fostered by the democratic teaching of the board school which—if it had accomplished nothing else—had effectually taught the children to be RUDE. The pretty simplicity and deferential mannerism described as characteristics of these villagers by mid-Victorian writers had become obsolete; courtseying was now regarded as *infra dig*: no one touched their hats to or moved aside for ladies, and the colloquial 'sir' and 'mam' had long since given place to a familiar and condescending 'Mr.' or 'Mrs.' as the case might be.

"In Cornwall, we were informed, the manners of the people are even worse, and if that is a fact, one can hardly believe it possible, I am quite certain we shall never cross the Tamar.

"Fortunately we had taken two of our favourite servants with us, namely, Marie and Eugenie—the latter my mother's own maid, a capable person who could turn her hand to anything, the former a clever little cook we had imported from our own country. But for this foresight on my part, I do not know how my mother could have managed to exist.

"She is even more fastidious than I. She cannot bear anything coarse or uncouth—in comparison a local servant would have made purgatory seem pleasant.

"I am afraid you will conclude we are rather hard to please: perhaps we are somewhat exacting, but we cannot help it; we are women of the old school, may I add, of gentle birth, who claim to the full all the privileges of our sex and station; besides we offered a good sum for the house: we expected to be treated fairly.

"According to the advertisement, 'The Hall' was furnished: it was, in reality, nothing of the sort. Can any house in which there is neither bookcase nor bathroom be said to be furnished? Though standing alone on a fairly large piece of ground—I cannot truthfully say a garden—it might well have been called semi-detached, for we searched in it in vain to find a whole piece of furniture.

"Marie and Eugenie are smart young women: they pride themselves on being slim and elegant. Imagine then their disgust when the kitchen chairs actually collapsed under them.

"I, too, had a grievance. Without conceit I may say that it is not in my nature to be clumsy. How was it then that I broke three cups, a saucer, and a cream-jug within the short space of half an hour? The reason was obvious enough! The cups were all cracked, the saucers damaged, and the jugs should have been labelled 'beware of the handle.' Even moderately disfigured china is my mother's pet aversion. How she suffered under these circumstances I will not attempt to describe.

"But the plate! I have heard of gold plate, silver plate, copper plate, brass plate, and electro plate, but with none of these could I associate this mongrel species, these odds and ends we were called upon to use. It was, indeed, an enigma, and I hate enigmas, especially when they are not worth the trouble of solving. Luckily, substitutes were easily obtainable. I wired for a complete supply of plate from home, after which the motley crew of hirelings were no longer in evidence.

"And the carpets! I have always thought such luxuries, even the most costly, a doubtful blessing; these were undoubtedly an unmixed evil. Fortunately, we were able to dispense with them. The floors underneath were of polished oak, and with these we were greatly taken. True, we were somewhat puzzled to account for certain irregularities in the boards, but, on the whole, I think we should have been more astonished had we found them intact.

"Could we, by any means, make the place tenantable? Marie and Eugenie are brave and forgiving girls! In spite of their recent adventure—they had never been so insulted in their lives—they thought it possible; mother and I were doubtful.

"We hired all the furniture there was to be hired from the village, we engaged by the day the only prepossessing and respectable woman it contained, and we tried to settle down and pretend we enjoyed it. From the beginning it was a fiasco—we were miserable! and to add to our distress, or rather, to fill to overflowing our cup of misfortune, the weather became miserable, too; it began to rain.

"What was there to hope for now? Nothing! What was there to do now? Nothing! Nothing but sit at the window and gaze at the dreary lawn, shut off from the road by a hideous wall, or to flit about from room to room wringing one's hands like a distracted phantom.

"A phantom! I did not believe in phantoms when I came to Thurlow; I treated the Unknown with the blind levity of a Voltaire; I was inconsequently sceptical; I had been born psychic.

"Though I was sublimely unconscious of it, the dawn of my awakening was at hand.

"Though the house was undesirable in so many ways—cold, bare, comfortless, dilapidated—it was not without interest. It was old—old with the antiquity of two or more centuries—and age is always interesting.

"There were rooms in it, narrow, rectangular rooms darkened by Virginian creeper that dropped their crimson foliage over diamond panes, rooms the very air of which seemed charged with the shades of old-world wits and *savants*.

"In my imagination the house had once been a school: the severity of the walls, the coldness of their neat yellow stones suggested it; I even went so far as to fancy I could discern ink-stains on the skirting-boards; and who but schoolboys ever desecrate a floor with ink-stains?

"The predominating feature in the house was undoubtedly the staircase.

"It was the first thing one noticed on entering; there was no escaping it. Confronting the door in the very middle of the hall, it stood there like some grey and massive sentinel—and barred the way. One wondered how it had ever got there, it was so disproportionately large for the house. It was masterful, aggressive, FASCINATING (Marie declared 'there was no getting away from it—that it LIVED')—and—it was made of STONE. There was no doubt about it now 'The Hall' had indeed been a school; would any one but a pedagogue have a stone staircase? Eugh! my mother felt a twinge of rheumatism the moment she set eyes on it.

"It was curiously wanting in proportion; consisting of barely a dozen steps, it was most uncomfortably steep and of a most unnecessary width. I compared it with some strange, squatting animal—a comparison that grew on me the longer I remained in the house.

"At the top of the staircase was a gallery, protected by high rails, which I discovered connected the used and disused portions of the house. In the latter there were some rooms we did not care to inhabit; there were a few we were even unable to explore—they were locked.

"I felt no curiosity about them; they were certain to be both commonplace, prosaic and dusty: every time I passed them I smelt dust—and I cannot endure a particle of dust. If I had believed any of them to be a library, I might have been tempted to pick the lock; I am passionately fond of books—that is to say, of some books—when I am exiled in the country and it is always raining.

"I was in search of a book which I had laid down somewhere, when I crossed the hall one afternoon, and left my mother dozing in a big armchair before the drawing-room fire.

"Marie said she had seen it on the oak settle; most likely, for I often took my book and lounged on it. You see I had grown fond of the oak settle naturally, for it was the only piece of furniture in that monster house that stirred in me any friendly feeling whatever. But Marie must have been dreaming, it was certainly not there. I would have called to Marie to come and help me search for it, had I not remembered that she and Eugenie had gone into the village to do a little shopping on their own account. They laugh in their grandest manner at those 'silly little shops,' but with a true woman's instinct they cannot resist 'buying.'

"I felt indignant, provoked, angry! never had I wanted to read so much and never had I been at such a loss to find a book.

"Oh! I recollected there was one upstairs—an ancient and musty edition of 'Eugene Aram'—(proof positive, this, that the place was once a school; would any one save a schoolmaster read 'Eugene Aram')? I had seen it lying on the floor of a disused cupboard—alone and forsaken: a solitary relic of the Academical bookshelf.

"Were I in a library, 'Eugene Aram' would probably be the last book I would choose to read; Lytton's tales are horrible; I abominate horrors. I thought of the staircase, I glanced at it; it was really very dark. I shuddered!

"I did not understand why I shuddered, unless it was on account of a draught! Of course, a draught. The house was full of draughts. The hour was late, the afternoon was cold, it was March, and undoubtedly a door was open somewhere; the book was not worth the trouble, I was over-tired, I would return to my mother. This I was actually preparing to do when the sudden appearance of a light made me pause—it came from the disused wing overhead.

"I can assure you I wanted very much to go to my mother; I would have given all I possessed to have gone to my mother; I could not: I could not stir; that light enthralled me.

"I had never seen such a light—such a queer, unaccountable light—a light that to anyone less sceptical might have seemed an 'UNNATURAL' Light! Perhaps it was an unnatural light—and I laughed. But what—what in the name of Heaven could it be?

"Drawing rapidly nearer and quickly assuming the appearance and proportions of a FIRE, it filled me with the most unusual, the most preposterously unusual, doubts and fears.

"And now for the first time I detected it was accompanied by incongruous though perfectly intelligible sound—the sound of someone tapping with all their might, tapping with a pair of high-heeled shoes.

"Aghast at this discovery, my perplexities increased, and I was vainly endeavouring to extricate myself from a chaotic quagmire of unpleasant thoughts, when a scream, the very intensity of which made me tremble, echoed and re-echoed throughout the house.

"'Fire! Fire! Bring me Fire!' These words, apparently so strangely paradoxical, were repeated with renewed vigour and anguish, the voice after each effort dying away into the most appalling and piteous wail.

"The screams were coming nearer, but before I had time to realise the tumult was so close at hand, or to fortify myself against the tableau I now had every reason to anticipate, a girl, her hair and dress a mass of lurid flames, came rushing frantically into the gallery.

"The spectacle she presented was so satanically awful that I immediately crossed myself. An indescribable thrill of terror ran through me. I felt—I KNEW—I was actually in the presence of an apparition; nothing 'earthly' could possibly have produced a similar or in any way equivalent effect.

"Staring at me through the yellow inferno of flames was a woman's face that, despite its horribly contorted features, was amazingly and uniquely beautiful, the perfect regularity of the Jewish lineaments being strikingly enhanced by the whiteness of the teeth, the blueness of the eyes.

"The latter came upon me as a further shock. Though very lovely both in their excessive length and hue, they did not match that style of face; to have done so they should have been black or brown—and their expression was repellent.

"I say repellent; I might with great accuracy say 'hellish,' for I saw in them the mirror of a sinful soul—of a VERY sinful soul.

"I could form no idea as to her dress, the blaze effectually hid everything save her face; but from the partial glimpse I caught of a pair of satin shoes, I surmised she was in some sort of ball-room costume. The duration of her transit, though to me an eternity, could not, I fancy, have occupied more than a very few seconds.

"Still gazing at me and beating the air with its hands, the phantom rushed shrieking onwards, disappearing with the impetus of a tornado in the inhabited portion of the house.

"I had no further 'use' for 'Eugene Aram.' I returned to my mother.

"The same phenomena was witnessed by Marie and Eugenie respectively within the next three days—on the fourth we left. Had we remained, there might have been a fatality; we were all genuinely frightened—and mother is an invalid—a very nervous invalid.

"Perhaps you feel inclined to say it was all a matter of nerves. What more likely! We were an isolated quartet of over-imaginative women! Or you might say that some story we had heard in connection with the house suggested these occult demonstrations.

"Do not be premature! We only heard a few weeks ago that 'The Hall' had a reputation for being haunted, and it is now several months since we left Thurlow. Our informant, a former tenant, was, we have every reason to believe, a person of indisputable veracity and common sense, in short, a person quite incapable of inventing any such story as the following which he kindly narrated for our satisfaction.

"It appears from what he told us (his MS. is still in my bureau) that Thurlow Hall once belonged to Mrs. Purvis, an old lady with one child, Charles.

"Charles was, of course, the apple of her eye; Charles ruled the house; every one must obey Mr. Charles; Mr. Charles could do nothing wrong. Nothing wrong until, in the heyday of his youth, in the season of wild oats, he unexpectedly fell in love with a Gaiety girl—Phyllis (no one remembered her other name)—and married her—and THAT was very wrong.

"His mother was indignant—FURIOUS—not with Charles, of course—but with that creature—Phyllis.

"Phyllis had inveigled him into marrying her; Phyllis would bring eternal disgrace on the family; Phyllis would run away with another man and ruin him.

"Ruin HIM—ruin Charles—and the fond mother grew despondent, very despondent, so despondent indeed that unkind neighbours said she was mad. They were wrong; the despondency was only a reaction, she suddenly cheered up, all was apparently forgiven and forgotten. Charles and Phyllis were invited to spend Christmas at Thurlow.

"They went, very naturally they went—Charles overjoyed at the prospect of displaying the Purvis estate to his charming wife.

"His mother welcomed Phyllis effusively; she made her feel thoroughly at home; she expressed an ardent desire to see her in her bridal robes.

"Phyllis consented—what else could she do? She had been a Gaiety girl! she had lived for admiration.

"Arrayed in her wedding garments she entered Mrs. Purvis's room, surprising the old lady in the act of lighting an oil lamp—a rather 'shaky' old lamp filled to the brim with oil.

"Phyllis was radiant; her sole thought was of the sensation she would create at the coming Christmas festivities. Had she been less absorbed she might have noticed how the hand trembled that raised the lamp; she might even have been on her guard.

"But vanity as well as love is blind. Phyllis accepted Mrs. Purvis's profuse expressions of admiration and delight in good faith; they were, of course, both genuine and natural; they were, moreover, her due. The bride was intent on examining herself in the mirror; her mother-in-law approached her from behind, and, bending suddenly forward, deliberately hurled the lamp on to the train of her dress. There was a loud crash—an explosion—and the wedding dress was on fire.

"No one was at hand to render assistance, Charles and the servants having been slyly inveigled out of the house, and the only response to her screams were loud peals of laughter from her now wholly insane mother-in-law.

"It was small wonder that the poor girl lost her head, and, craving water, cried in her agony, 'Bring me fire, oh! bring me fire!'

"In that mad rush from the room along the disused corridors her one endeavour would appear to have been to reach her bedroom—perhaps she had forgotten that Charles had gone OUT—but her efforts were frustrated by the fiendish fury of the flames. The amount of oil on her dress must have made it blaze like a furnace.

"She had barely crossed the gallery into the opposite wing of the house before her scorched and smouldering limbs gave way, and falling to the ground she was speedily burned to ashes; her supreme and final agony being summed up in a despairing cry, so loud and piercing that it was even heard outside by Charles.

"Not daring to approach the house alone, Charles summoned some villagers, and keeping well in their rear, gingerly accompanied them across the lawn to the front entrance.

"There they were met by Mrs. Purvis, chuckling horribly.

"Corridors, gallery and staircase were in flames, and had it not been for the opportune arrival of the vicar the whole place would have been consumed; thanks, however, to his vigour and level-headedness the fire was eventually extinguished, and although the damage done was considerable, the bulk of the property remained unscathed.

"No trace of the unfortunate Mrs. Charles Purvis being found, the precise manner of her death for many years remained a mystery. But the erratic babblings of her mother-in-law supplied material for certain conjectures, which were afterwards confirmed by the lucid and exhaustive confession of the old lady, who regained her reason on her deathbed.

"Though a thorough restoration of the property was effected, Charles would never live at the Hall. A long series of unsatisfactory tenancies succeeded the events I have just related, and the story of a ghost has at length come to stay.

"N.B.—I have good reason for believing the house is still (August 1908) haunted; most probably this will always be the case."

□□□

THE GUILSBOROUGH GHOST

OR A

MINUTE ACCOUNT[4] OF THE APPEARANCE OF

THE GHOST OF

JOHN CROXFORD

EXECUTED AT NORTHAMPTON, AUGUST 4, 1764

For the Murder of a Stranger

in the Parish of GUILSBOROUGH

Printed in the year 1764 and reprinted by

F. Cordeaux, Northampton, 1819

PART I

Technical form of apparition: Phantasm of dead

Source of authenticity: Copied almost *ad verbum* from the above MS., lent me by a resident in Guilsborough, August 5, 1908

Cause of Haunting: Murder

PREFACE

THE publication from which the following extracts are taken was printed at Northampton (where the original may still be seen, August 1908) in the year 1764.

It appears that the author, who was officiating there as temporary chaplain to the jail, was a man of indisputable and well-known integrity, and a very popular preacher throughout the county.

In order to render his work useful and instructive, innumerable references are made to the Scriptures, but his quotations are of too great a length for the following abridged tract, which is copied from the original and contains only the account of the interview the author had with Croxford's Ghost.

THE GHOST

It appears from the account given in a pamphlet reprinted and sold by G. Henson, Letterpress and Copper-plate Printer, Bridge Street, Northampton, 1848, that on Saturday, August 4, 1764, John Croxford, together with three others of the names of Seamark, Deacon and Butlin were tried at the Assizes of Northampton and convicted of murder.

It came out at the trial that the unfortunate victim was a native of Scotland, travelling with goods, and that by chance he called at the house of Seamark, a shepherd's hut in the parish of Guilsborough, Northamptonshire, where Croxford and his companions used to meet, where they robbed and afterwards cruelly murdered him, and in order to prevent a discovery consumed his body in an oven; which was proved on the evidence of one of Seamark's children, who was an eye-witness to the transaction, by looking through the crevices of the floor from the room above.

They were all found guilty and executed on August 4, 1764, and Croxford's body hung in chains on Hollowell Heath, in the parish of Guilsborough, near the spot where the horrid deed was perpetrated—(and no spot more suggestive of such a tragedy could be imagined).

The author of the work—at that time (1764) holding the appointment of chaplain to the Northampton Jail—after quoting passages from various writers to prove the reality of the subject, proceeds to give an account of the appearance of Croxford's Ghost, as follows:

"I shall now proceed without further lett or impediment to a plain and conscientious account of the ghost or apparition which was the occasion of my troubling the world with this narrative; unless I first observe that the behaviour of the prisoners, one of whom is the subject of these pages, lately tried, condemned and executed at Northampton, for the murder of a person unknown, upon the evidence of Ann Seamark and her son, about nine or ten years old, was such as astonished every beholder....

"Clear and conclusive as the evidence was against them, no arguments, even after condemnation, though delivered and enforced with the utmost energy, precision and perspicuity by a learned and worthy divine, were able to reach their hardened hearts and prevail for an open and unreserved confession of their guilt. Even at the gallows, in their last addresses to the people, they insisted on their innocence in the strongest terms imaginable; wishing the heaviest penalties an offended God could inflict might be their portion in the next world, if they were guilty of the murder that was laid to their charge and for which they were about to suffer.

"Thus did they divide the sentiments of the crowd that many were brought over to a full persuasion of their innocence, while others were left halting between two opinions and severely agitated with conflicting doubts. But mark the event.

"After having instructed my people as a teacher in the knowledge of the Scriptures, I used to spend the superfluous hours of the Lord's Day in perusing some part or other of the Old and New Testament.

"Accordingly, on August 12, 1764, being the Sabbath, I returned as usual into my study, the door of which is secured by a lock with a spring-bolt, and sat down to my accustomed evening devotion; the business of this day by rotation laying in the New Testament, and in that part of it where St. Paul in his Epistle to the Corinthians proposes, maintains and proves the resurrection of the body. Struck with the sublimity of his thoughts, boldness of his figures, and energy of his diction, and convinced by the number and weight of his arguments, and looking with a pleasing foretaste of happiness into futurity, I was on a sudden surprised with the perfect form and appearance of a man, who stood erect at a small distance from my right side.

"Conscious that the door was locked and that there was no other means by which my visitor could have entered, I was considerably surprised—surprise turning into abject terror—when, glancing with irresistible fascination at the man, I perceived in him something indefinably but most unmistakably Unnatural.

"Feeling sure that I was in the actual presence of an apparition, I contrived, by an almost superhuman effort, I admit, to sum up sufficient courage to speak—my voice seeming dry and unrecognisable.

"I addressed it in the power and spirit of the Gospel; inquiring on what errand it was sent; what was intended by such an application, and what services could be expected from a person of so little note and mean abilities as myself.

"I must here state that although the spectre had inspired me with so much awe, I did not associate it with anything EVIL.

"Every second tended to strengthen my composure, and when it spoke in a voice rather more hollow and intense, perhaps, than that of a human being, my fears were instantly dissipated. I was now able to take a close stock of it, and observed that in features, general appearance, and clothes it closely resembled any ordinary labouring man; it was in expression and colouring, only it differed—its eyes were lurid, its cheeks livid.

"Raising one extremely white and emaciated hand, it desired me to compose myself, saying that as it was now strictly limited by a Superior Power, and could do no one act but by the permission of God, I had no reason to be afraid, abrupt as was its appearance, and that if I would endeavour to overcome the visible perturbation I was in, it would proceed in the business of its errand.

"At this announcement my heart fluttered with an excitement I found difficult to control. Was the wonderful mystery that had hitherto enshrouded the existence and composition of the Unknown about to be revealed to me—was I going to be initiated into those secrets heretofore denied to man? Eagerly promising to compose myself, and lost to all else save the fascinating presence of my guest, I settled down to listen to anything the phantasm might have to say.

"The room, I must here state, was lighted by a single, though rather powerful, double-wick oil lamp, which I had always deemed sufficient to illuminate the whole apartment, but which now—and I could not help noticing the phenomenon—did not extend its rays beyond the cadaverous face of my intruder, upon which the full force of its light seemed concentrated.

"Commencing in clear and solemn tones, the phantasm stated that it was one of the unhappy prisoners executed at Northampton on the 4th of August, 1764.

"A cold chill ran down my back at this announcement, which was intensified when I recognised for the first time that the figure confronting me bore a startling likeness to one of the prisoners it had been my unhappy lot to address prior to his execution: there was the same hair, brows and beard—black and stubby; the protruding forehead and retreating chin that had so repelled me, the malshaped head and the broken, unsavoury-looking teeth; it was indeed the ghost of one of those diabolical miscreants that stood before me, and, despite the fact that I was brought up in the strict Protestant faith, I inadvertently crossed myself.

"The spectre went on without apparently heeding my action.

"'It had been,' so it proclaimed, 'the principal and ringleader of the gang, most of whom it had corrupted, debauched and seduced to that deplorable method of life, and it was particularly appointed by Providence to undeceive the world and remove those doubts which the solemn protestations of their innocence to the very hour of death had raised in the minds of all who heard them.'

"At this juncture, excitement overcoming fear and aversion, I hazarded to inquire of the phantasm its name.

"Its reply, delivered in the same slow, measured, almost mechanical tones (as if it were only the mouth-organ of some other and unseen agency) was to the effect that its name was John Croxford; that it had express directions to come to me—directions it could not disobey; it furthermore explained the reason the murderers had so persistently insisted on their innocence, lay in the fact, that, while the blood of their victim was still warm, they entered into a sacramental obligation, which they sealed by dipping their fingers in the blood of the deceased and licking the same, by which they bound themselves under the penalty of eternal damnation never to betray the fact themselves nor to confess, if condemned to die for it on the evidence of others, and that they were further encouraged to such measures, since, as Seamark himself was a confederate in the murder, they concluded the evidence of his wife would not be admitted; that as the child was so young, they presumed no judge or jury would pay the least regard to his depositions; that as Butlin had but lately entered into a confederacy with them, and no robberies could be readily proved against him, they thought it would appear impossible for one of his age to begin a career of wickedness with murder (it being observed in a proverb that no man is abandoned all at once); that if they could invalidate the evidence on behalf of Butlin it must be of equal advantage to them all; that though disappointed of this view in court and condemned to die upon the above evidence, they were still infatuated with the same notion even at the gallows, and expected a reprieve for Butlin when the halter was about his neck, and consequently, if such a reprieve had been granted, as the evidence was as full and decisive against Butlin as against them, the sentence for the murder must have been withdrawn from all, their execution deferred, and perhaps transportation only their final punishment."

Though listening to every word with abnormal attention, I became at the same time aware of a strange and uncanny feeling that the identity of the phantasm was but partly revealed to me in the corpse-like figure opposite; what its true and entire nature might be I dared not even hazard a conjecture.

In the pause that followed its last speech, more to hear myself speak than anything else (I could not endure the silence of THIS THING), I asked if the evidence of the woman and child was clear, punctual and particular; to which it replied, "It was as circumstantial, distinct and methodical as possible; varying not in the least from truth in any one particular of consequence, unless in the omission of their horrid sacrament which she might possibly neither observe nor know."

I then asked why they had behaved with such impropriety, impudence and clamour upon their trial; to which it replied, "that they had been somewhat elevated with liquor, privately conveyed to them, and that by effrontery and a seemingly undaunted behaviour they hoped to intimidate the WOMAN, throw her into confusion, perplex her depositions, thereby rendering the evidence precarious and inconclusive, or at least give the court some favourable presumptions of their innocence."

I next inquired whether they knew the name of the person murdered, whence he came, and what reasons they had for committing so horrid a barbarity.

To which the phantasm answered, "that the man was a perfect stranger to them all, that the murder was committed more out of wantonness and the force of long-contracted habits of wickedness than necessity, as they were at that time in no want of money; that they first found occasion to quarrel with the pedlar through a strange propensity to mischief for which it could not account but from God's withdrawing His grace, and leaving them to all the extravagance and irregularities of a corrupted heart, long hardened in the ways of sin; that the man, being stout and undaunted, resented their ill-usage, and in his own defence proceeded to blows; that two only—Deacon and Croxford—were at first concerned, but finding him resolute, they had called up Seamark and Butlin, who were at a distance behind the hedge; that they then all seized the pedlar, notwithstanding which he struggled with great violence to the very last against their united efforts; nor did they think it safe to trifle any longer with a man who gave such proofs of uncommon strength; that with much difficulty they dragged him down to Seamark's yard and there committed the murder as represented in court."

I next asked if there was any licence in his bags or pockets, that they might discover his name or place of abode.

It replied, "No! that the paper left behind in its (Croxford's) writing was of a piece with the rest of their conduct in this affair, a hardened untruth, abounding with reflections as false, as scandalous and wicked, suggested by the Father of Lies, who had gradually brought them from one step of iniquity to another, beginning first in the violation of morality, to the place of purgatory in which they now were."

It further declared (a statement that interested me greatly), "That though their bodies were unaffected with pain, their souls were in darkness, under all the dreadful apprehensions of remaining there for eternity, far beyond what the liveliest imagination while influenced by the weight and grossness of matter, can conceive; that their doom had been not a little aggravated by their final impenitence, impiety and profaneness in adjuring God by the most horrid imprecations to attest the truth of a palpable and notorious falsehood, and by wishing that their own portion in Eternity might be determined in consequence thereof. Language," the apparition said, "was too weak to describe and mortality incapable of conceiving a ten-thousandth part of their anguish and despair even at present, and happy would it be for succeeding ages if Posterity could be induced to profit by their misfortunes and be influenced by this account to avoid the punishment of the Earthbound."

All this the phantasm delivered with such increased distinction and perspicuity, with such an emphasis and tone of voice, as plainly evinced the truth of what it spoke and claimed my closest attention and regard; and as it seemed to hint that I was singled out to acquaint the world with these particulars I told it that the present age was one of incredulity and agnosticism, that few gave credit to fables of this kind, that the world would conclude me either a madman or impostor or brand me with the odious imputations of superstition and enthusiasm, that, therefore, true credentials would be necessary, not only to preserve my own character, but also to procure respect and credit to my relations.

To this the phantasm instantly responded that what I observed was perfectly right and requisite to authenticate the truth of this affair, and that unless some proper attestations were given to accounts of this nature, they would be considered by the rational part of mankind as mere tales, invented only to amuse the credulous or frighten children on a winter's evening into temper and obedience; in short, that they would have no weight, and disappoint the ends of Providence, who intends them for the good and benefit of the world; that, therefore, in order to encourage my perseverance in supporting the truth of this appearance and embolden me to publish a minute detail of it, it would direct me to such a criterion as would put the reality of it beyond all dispute; and it accordingly told me that in such a spot, describing it as minutely as possible, in the parish of Guilsborough, was deposited a gold ring which belonged to the pedlar whom they murdered, and moreover in the inside was engraved this singular motto:

HANGED HE'LL BE WHO STEALS ME, 1745

"That on perusing it," the apparition continued, "it (Croxford) had been smitten with grave apprehensions, and, thinking the words ominous, had buried the ring, hoping thus to elude the sentence denounced at random against the unlawful possessor of it, and even escape the vindictive justice of Heaven itself by such a precaution; that if I found not every particular in regard to this ring exactly as it related it to me, then I might conclude there was not a single syllable of truth in the whole, and consequently no obligation lay upon me to take any further concerns in the affair."

Engaged in this interesting and all-absorbing conversation, I suddenly became aware it was very late—the silence throughout the house for the first time appalled me, and I was about to make a movement towards the door to make sure all was safe without, when the light from the lamp once again became normal. With a startled glance I looked for the phantasm—it was gone; nor was there any other means by which it could have taken its departure save by dematerialisation.

Bitterly disappointed, my fears being now entirely removed, at so abrupt a disappearance, I sat down very calmly, and in the coolest manner canvassed over the whole matter to myself, reflected seriously on every particular, and was induced to conclude from the coherence and punctuality of the account that it was impossible it should be fiction or imposture. I laid particular stress upon the circumstance of the ring, the singularity of its motto, and the minute description of the spot where it was deposited.

I considered, moreover, from the tests I had made by shutting my eyes and pressing the balls with my forefinger, that I had been perfectly awake, had had the full use both of my senses and reason, and was as capable of knowing the figure and voice of a man as the size and print of the book I was reading at the time the ghost made its appearance.

In short, firmly persuaded of the truth of what I had heard and seen, I resolved on the morrow to search for the ring, and thereby clear it up beyond all possibility of doubt.

Accordingly on Monday morning early, between four and five o'clock, I set out alone, making directly to the spot the phantasm had described; found the ring without the least difficulty or delay; examined the motto and date of it, which corresponded exactly with his account of it, and fully convinced me of my obligation to communicate to the world the particulars of the whole.

With this resolution, immediately on my return I sat down and drew up the whole conversation as near as I could recollect, neither omitting nor adding any circumstance of consequence in the manner you now see it, and trusting it will prove of use to the public for whose benefit it seems intended.

The original manuscript, to which the author appends his name, concludes with a very fervid exhortation to piety, coupled with an equally strong warning against indulgence in vice and crime.

The story of the ghost, judging by the interest that is even now (1908) taken in it, must have created a considerable sensation at the time—so much so that I think a brief history of the crime—gruesome though it be—will bear repeating.

Prior to doing so, however, I should like to relate a ghostly experience that happened to me, Elliott O'Donnell, in the same neighbourhood, August 1904.

The village of Guilsborough is on an eminence 10 miles N.W. by N. of Northampton, 4 miles from the source of the Avon at Naseby, 10 miles N.E. from Daventry, 11 miles from Lutterworth, 10 miles S.S.W. from Market Harboro', 12 miles E. from Rugby, and 76 miles from London.

The adjacent country, consisting of large stretches of smiling meadows, dales, and table-lands, is very fair for the eye to dwell upon, and it is only at night, when the shadows from the many spinneys are cast upon the gleaming roads and silent tarns, or when the wind, rustling through the elms and oaks, sound like the breaking and falling of surf on the seashore—it is only then that the place presents an entirely different aspect to the psychic mind and one conjures up—GHOSTS.

During the period of my early visits to Guilsborough, the history of the village was unknown to me, nor did I for one moment associate it with superphysical manifestations till I was staying at the hamlet of Creaton, some three miles distant, and had to tramp home late at night.

I must confess, then, that I was unquestionably glad to leave the crossroads at the top of Crow Hill and the lonely turnpike behind and find myself snugly ensconced within the very material precincts of the Cricketers' Arms.

The route I took, led me past the long-disused burial-ground of some Nonconformist Fraternity, a spot one never seemed to notice by day, but which struck me as singularly eerie at night.

On this particular night in question, I did not leave my friend's house in Guilsborough till close on twelve, an hour when all village folk are in bed and the place is wrapped in the most profound silence. The sound of my footsteps, as I briskly pounded down the road, echoed and re-echoed through the village. I welcomed the sound; it was nice to have even that for a companion. I am not as a rule nervous, I have been too much by myself in life to be an abject coward, yet I must confess I never anticipated the walk from Guilsborough along the lonely turnpike-road after nightfall without an uncomfortable itching in my back.

I was just beginning to get that sensation when I arrived at the rusty gates of the cemetery, and was confounded beyond measure on seeing a curious, grotesque sort of creature climb over the iron bars and confront me. The moonlight was so powerful that it left nothing uncovered or concealed.

A frightful terror laid hold of me—what—what in the NAME OF HEAVEN could it be?

Gazing at it with a fascination as hideous as the thing itself, I took in every feature—the long, loose limbs, the thin body, the huge hands and feet, the little repulsive head, the white fulsome, pig-like face, and the protruding, sapphire eyes.

For some seconds—to me an eternity—we watched one another in breathless silence—the Elemental (for as such I at length recognised it) being the first to take the initiative. The unfathomable stare in its eyes gradually deepened into a horrible and very unmistakable expression of malignant joy in which all the most undesirable of human vices seemed blended: its monstrous hands rose like wings on either side of its head, the fingers twitching convulsively in greedy anticipation of clutching me; its legs slowly crouched as if about to spring—and then—just as the crucial moment arrived and the acme of my terrors was reached—the spell was broken—the leaden weights fell from off my feet—my limbs became endowed with a thousandfold their natural elasticity—and—turning round—I fled.

So ended my first and only experience with a Guilsborough ghost. I have taken very good care since then to give that burial-ground a very wide berth after nightfall. But now comes the most extraordinary part of it. I had heard off-and-on that a certain house in the village (since pulled down) was supposed to be haunted; that one bedroom in particular had struck those occupying it as containing an invisible "presence" both inimical and horrible.

I never, however, associated this mysterious something with the Elemental I had seen, till, in the course of a conversation with an old and highly respected inhabitant of the village a few days since (August 10, 1908), I learned that he had had a psychical adventure of a somewhat extraordinary nature in his boyhood.

Upon pressing him, he told me that he had lived in the haunted house as a child, and on running upstairs to his bedroom one morning had seen a long, thin human form with a tiny head and animal's face crouching on the bed and staring at him. Terrified out of his wits by this unexpected and startling spectacle, he had remained glued to the spot for some seconds, until a slight movement on the part of the Elemental broke the spell, and he was able to "bolt" precipitately from the apartment: this was the only time he saw it.

Here then surely was the key to the nature of the haunting—an Elemental or Poltergeist, assuredly the same that had appeared to me some fifty years later at the gate of the old burial-ground.

My informant, by the way, had not heard of my experience; I had told it to no one: hence this visual occult manifestation of mine in Guilsborough stands corroborated.

But why this haunting? Why this form of apparition?

I dived into the history of Guilsborough, and discovered that quantities of fossils (trilobites, &c.), together with implements of flint—*i.e.*, arrow-heads, javelins, celts (the latter popularly known as "thunderbolts") have been and are still found in various parts of the village and in the gravel-pits of the adjoining hamlets of Nortorft and Hollowell; that tumuli yet remain in Guilsborough Park and in several of the neighbouring fields, and that numbers of very ancient bones have been from time to time dug out of the soil in all parts of the village.

All this is conclusive evidence that Guilsborough is far older than its average inhabitant of to-day imagines, that it has been alternately the site of Palaeolithic and Neolithic settlements, and that all sorts of barbaric rites and ceremonies have been conducted on the very ground where houses and cottages now stand.

Hence it is not very surprising to any one at all versed in the *modus operandi* of Phantasms and Psychic Phenomena to hear that one of the apparitions (at least) haunting Guilsborough appears in the form of a sub-human or sub-animal elemental.

Superphysical manifestations of this kind—let me explain for the benefit of the inexperienced—usually occur on the sites of or near ancient and unconsecrated or long-disused burial-places—the whys and the wherefores of which I hope to dwell upon in detail in a subsequent volume.

PART II

I now append the account of the Croxford Trial copied (with as few alterations as possible) from the pamphlet reprinted by Mr. Henson of Northampton in 1848

AT the Assizes held at Northampton on Thursday, August 2, 1764, came on before the Right Honourable the Lord Chief Baron Varker the trials of Benjamin Deacon, John Croxford, and Richard Butlin for the murder of a travelling pedlar—known only as Scottie—at a house of ill-fame called "Catslo"—in the Parish of Guilsborough, kept by one Thomas Seamark (who was executed at Northampton on April 23 last for a robbery on the highway) and had been a receptacle of thieves and highwaymen for some time.

The chief evidence against them was that of Anne Seamark, widow of the above Thomas Seamark. She deposed that sometime between Michaelmas and Christmas last the said pedlar (supposed to be one Thomas Corey) came to the said house where were at that time the said Seamark, Deacon, Croxford, and Butlin to whom he offered stockings, &c., for sale, but not agreeing as to the price, they proposed to murder him and directly Seamark knocked him down, Butlin fell upon his legs, Deacon upon his face to prevent him crying out and Croxford, pulling out a knife, cut his throat in such a manner that the head was almost off, but the body stirring a little, Croxford stabbed him in the head which put an end to his life.

They then stripped him and carried the clothes upstairs where Seamark's three children were in bed; after which a hole was dug by Seamark in the close adjoining to the house where they buried the body; but thinking themselves not safe, they dug up the body again and cut it into several pieces.

These latter they put into an oven and were three days and nights trying to consume them; in the end succeeding only with the flesh and having to bury the bones which were now produced in court and held as testimony against them.

Being asked by the judge why she did not reveal the same before, Mrs. Seamark answered that her husband threatened to murder her if she mentioned it to anyone, whilst Croxford holding a knife to her throat with one hand and having a book in the other, swore he would instantly kill her if she did not take an oath to conceal all knowledge of the matter.

The next witness for the prosecution, Mrs. Seamark's little boy of ten years of age, stated that on being kicked one day at school by a playmate, he had in a passion cried out that he would serve him as his daddy served "Scottie," which statement being overheard by the schoolmaster, the latter called him into his presence and demanded an explanation.

On the witness refusing to comply, he was shut in a room by himself where he remained till the arrival of his mother.

In the meantime the Schoolmaster, who like everyone else in Guilsborough, had only known the Pedlar by the name of "Scottie," and like other folk had wondered at his long absence from the village, seeing that many people owed him money and others were in want of goods, began to put two and two together and had arrived at the conclusion that the boy knew more than he dare tell, when Mrs. Seamark entered the house in a state of breathless alarm to know why her son had not "turned up" for his dinner. Whereupon the Schoolmaster had boldly taxed her with a knowledge of Scottie's fate which after no little hesitation and a great many tears she had admitted.

This had led to the present witness confessing, that chancing to peep through the cracks of the chamber floor one afternoon, he had seen his father and some other men trying to burn some hands and feet in an oven, near to which were a light grey coat and a cane which he recognised as belonging to "Scottie" who had been to their house the day before. On being asked by the Judge if he could identify the prisoners with the men he had seen helping his father, he at once answered in the affirmative.

This concluded his testimony after which several other witnesses (whose evidence I cannot record here through lack of space) were then called; Croxford, Deacon and Butlin protesting their innocence of the crime laid against them, declaring that the whole case had been maliciously trumped up by Mrs. Seamark and her son.

After the evidence on both sides had been thoroughly examined, the judge summed up, and the jury after a quarter of an hour's absence returned with a verdict of wilful murder; a demonstration being made by the prisoners against Ann Seamark as she left the Court.

On Saturday August 4th, the prisoners were carried from the jail to the place of execution, guarded by a party of Sir Charles Howard's Dragoons with fixed bayonets and muskets loaded with powder and ball, where they joined fervently in the prayers with the minister, Croxford delivering a paper to one of the attendant gaolers, which he desired might be published for the satisfaction of the world. This document is too long to quote *ad verbum*; a brief summary will suffice. In it John Croxford says that he is about twenty-three years of age and by trade a tailor, that he was born at Brixworth of creditable parents who gave him a liberal education, and that his character and behaviour were very good until about January 1760, when he got into bad company, which had proved his ruin—this much he confessed, but denied that he had been guilty of murder.

Benjamin Deacon writes that he was born at Spratton, is about twenty-five years of age, and by trade a sawyer; that he bore a tolerably good character until about Christmas last, when he committed various crimes, but not murder.

Richard Butlin testifies that he was born of respectable parents at Guilsborough, had a good education, is about twenty years of age, and by trade a glover and breeches maker, that he has always borne a good character and is innocent of murder.

The manuscript goes on to say that they—the said John Croxford, Benj. Deacon and Richard Butlin—were to die the next day, being condemned on the false oath of Ann Seamark, the vilest wretch that ever appeared in a Court of Justice, and that there was not one word of truth in her evidence and that of her boy, it being a hellish and malicious contrivance of their's to take away their lives, that Croxford was never with Butlin until Guilsborough Feast, which was about the 25th of October, and never was in the Close with Butlin and Deacon but once, and that about the 15th of November, and never in the house with them; and that in their opinion no murder had been committed.

That they did not doubt but the whole affair would be brought to light, though too late to be of any service to them; and that they hoped Ann Seamark would be rewarded according to her deserts, that they would die in peace with her and with all the world, bearing her no malice, only hoping the great God would make known their innocence.

The document winds up with these words: "Done in Northampton Gaol, the night before the execution, as a caution to all good people. We, the poor unhappy sufferers, do severally set our hands to this, it being nothing but Truth,

"JOHN CROXFORD.
"BENJ. DEACON.
"RICHARD BUTLIN."

At the place of execution they behaved with great fortitude, still denying their knowledge of the murder, but confessing themselves guilty of many irregularities. They gave much attention to the Divine Service, and departed, advising all the spectators to beware of keeping bad company and declaring that they died in peace with the world.

After their execution the body of Croxford was carried to Hollowell Heath, in the parish of Guilsborough, where it was hanged in chains on a gibbet erected for that purpose, the bodies of Deacon and Butlin being delivered to a surgeon to be dissected.

This concludes the history of the Guilsborough murder, posterity concurring with the verdict of the jury and agreeing that there were sensible and useful grounds for the appearance of the Phantasm of the perjured Croxford to the Chaplain of the Northampton Jail.

WOLSEY ABBEY, NEAR GLOUCESTER

THE DREADFUL SMELL

Technical form of apparitions: Phantasms of the dead

Source of authenticity: Copies almost *ad verbum* from the MS. lent me by Mrs. Browne, February 1908.

Cause of haunting: Vice and Premature Burial

MY name is Elizabeth Rita Browne; I am a native of Birmingham and my husband, John Alexander is the rector of a small parish near Wolverhampton.

In the summer of 1900 my husband, who had long been ailing, never having properly recovered from an attack of typhoid, was obliged to take a holiday, engaging a locum to do his work.

Like the majority of clergymen, his stipend was not very large and we could not, consequently, afford to go to any expensive place. An advertisement in a well-known fashion gazette attracting our attention, we at once made inquiries, with the result that Wolsey Abbey became ours for three months at a practically nominal rent.

Of course it was in an extremely out-of-the-way spot; there was no railway within six miles and the neighbourhood was dull, flat and uninteresting; still we might have marvelled at getting it so absurdly cheap, had we not heard that money was of no object to the owner, who was a semi-millionaire.

We arrived early one evening in July; the sun was yet visible in the sky and its dying efforts would have enhanced the meanest rural beauty.

I cannot say we were comfortably impressed with the building; it was of course simply colossal compared with our own little home, but so grim and grey, so forlorn and forbidding, and withal so inhospitable, that a momentary fear seized me lest its leaden hued and crumbling walls should prove our winding-sheets.

The grounds, overgrown with every imaginable kind of weed that here attained Brobdingnagian dimensions, gently shelved down to the house, which lay in a minute valley, dank, damp and dismal; the funereal aspect being further augmented by clumps of giant pines and elms, the shadows from which were already beginning to wave phantastically on both walls and gables.

To our right, almost hidden by the thick foliage of the trees and luxuriant herbage, we espied the twinkling surface of a sheet of water which we subsequently learned was a tarn or lake of almost unfathomable depth and darkness.

The principal feature of the mansion seemed to be that of antiquity, of excessive antiquity, more particularly the Gothic monastic dome which, resting on Norman columns, formed the termination of the left wing, the right and central portion of the house dating back I believe to Henry VIIth's reign—though of this I have no positive proof.

The lapse of ages had wrought much discolouration, added to which was the disfigurement caused by lichens and minute fungi that, spreading over the whole exterior, hung in a fine tangled web-work from the eaves. But apart from this there were no very great dilapidations, the masonry remaining intact, whilst the woodwork, save for a few deep rents and indentures, seemed to be in an extraordinarily good state of repair.

The hand of nature had apparently been peremptorily and mysteriously arrested in its work of dissolution and decay.

The inside of the house, though not belying the mournful expectations we had formed from the exterior, drew from us all exclamations of wonder and admiration—never had we seen such magnificent oak panelling, nor such exquisitely carved ceilings, nor such vast stretches of tapestry (worn and faded though it was), whilst the ebon blackness of the floors, and the size and massiveness of the furniture, were what we had hitherto only associated with the grandeur of a palace or castle.

My daughters Mary and Eunice were charmed and impressed, and both my husband and I felt our misgivings rapidly diminish when a few minutes later we were enjoying a dainty and well-cooked supper in one of the large and stately reception rooms.

The first days of our sojourn there passed with the pleasant monotony of well-earned rest; we rambled through the long and straggling and seemingly interminable corridors of the house, and about the grounds and gardens, finding much to marvel at, much to envy.

In the day time the sun struggling feebly through the trellised panes of glass filled the rooms and passages with a crimson glow—a glow both warming and enriching, but at various times and in certain places startlingly and horribly suggestive of blood; the analogy struck me the more forcibly each day I observed it, so much so that I grew afraid to ascend the staircases—ALONE.

Mary and Eunice laughed at my misgivings; to them the house and surroundings were the quintessence of mediæval splendour and romance; they revelled in the grandeur of the interior trappings, in the freedom of the vast park and gardens; it was only after the third week that they, too, suddenly grew AFRAID.

But whereas my fears had been prompted by a comparison, a comparison which, however near and repellent, still remained a COMPARISON, theirs were generated by something which, although scarcely more tangible, was unmistakably REAL.

They were constantly assailed by a SMELL—a cold, icy cold, pungent, beastly smell, that would on some occasions approach them along a corridor or staircase, and at others steal surreptitiously behind them from some obscure nook or cranny.

It was foul, pestilential, inexplicable; they had never smelt anything like it before; it was nothing recognisable; it neither emanated from drainage nor from dead animals behind the skirting-boards; it was nauseous, suffocating, freezing—and—as if it lived—it MOVED.

From the moment they first became aware of its presence, their pleasure in the house ceased; all their time was now spent in the garden, but in that part of the garden only whence no view of the tarn could be obtained and where there were no trees.

Neither my husband nor I had encountered the Smell, but it was not very long before the servants did—and—one by one they LEFT, nor could we find any that were willing to take their place, the Abbey bearing a very evil reputation in the neighbourhood.

The question of our daughters' health began to cause us some anxiety; were we doing right in remaining in the house and exposing them to the danger of some serious malady? for although the origin of the Smell was a mystery, the effect of so horrible a stench could not prove otherwise than injurious.

We decided, therefore, to give up our tenancy at the expiration of another week, the idea of quitting such palatial quarters and retiring to the meanness of some petty villa or four-room cottage not disturbing us half so much as our inability to arrive at the cause of that Smell.

In the silence of the night, when no other sounds were to be heard, save the gentle beating of the branches against our window and the occasional hooting of an owl, we lay awake and wondered, wondered why it never came to us, but always to Mary and Eunice.

The house, I have said, was liberally furnished; both rooms and passages were covered with soft if somewhat faded carpets; there was no lack of tables, couches, chairs, &c., whilst the walls were adorned with pictures which, though darkened by dust and blistered by the sun, revealed the art of old and well-known masters; but it was the library that attracted and pleased us most.

There arranged methodically in the ample bookcases were volumes of every description; books of ancient lore, *Spectators*, *Tatlers*, Richardson's "Pamela," Defoe's "Moll of Flanders," Tyndale's Bible,

Dryden's and Gifford's Translations from the Classics, the Mysticisms of Swedenborg, Behmen and Plotinus and countless others, many, even of greater rarity and value, bound uniformly in those covers of rich Moroccan leather so characteristic of the seventeenth and eighteenth centuries.

One among all others had riveted our attention from the very first. I have already alluded to the peculiar and ghastly phenomenon produced by the sun's rays penetrating the coloured glass in the corridors and on the staircases; here it was even more pronounced though only very locally, the full force of the rays being focussed in the most startling manner on the metal clasp of a volume of stupendous size and apparently vast antiquity; the result being that whereas the entire book was bathed in a bloody halo, the others were left in a comparatively clear and normal light.

Appalled yet fascinated by this unaccountable anomaly, we had several times attempted to remove the volume in order to pry into its contents but we were unable to do so, owing, we imagined, to its having stuck or being fastened in some peculiar manner to the shelf—and we were afraid to use any great force for fear of damaging the cover; consequently our curiosity had to remain unsatisfied.

The night, however, preceding our departure from the Abbey (August 11) my husband had already left by a mid-day train, I was whiling away the few remaining hours in the study—Mary and Eunice being as I thought, engaged in packing—when—suddenly—I heard some one approach the door as if on tiptoe. The next moment there came a loud knock and the sonorous sound of the grandfather clock in the alcove beside me commencing to strike seven, the two noises were almost simultaneous.

Wondering who my visitor could be—our only servant, a woman from the nearest village, having left an hour ago—I smoothed my gown and walking hastily to the door threw it open.

As I did so a current of cold air, tainted with the most disgusting and detestable stench conceivable, sent me half staggering, half choking backwards, and I perceived standing on the threshold, not ten paces from me two figures of hellish horror. Featureless, fleshless, foul, clad in the tattered, rotted garments of a monk and nun, they confronted me motionless, silent, and then the voice of my Eunice attracting their attention, they slowly wheeled round and glided ghoulishly along the passage.

I gave one shriek of warning to Eunice as she hove in sight, carrying in her arms a tray of odds and ends for me to sort.

For a second or so she stood too petrified to move—and—then—as the THINGS appeared on the verge of touching her with their long, outstretched arms, she dropped the tray and, uttering a kind of terrified gasp, fled precipitately.

They did not pursue her, but gliding onward with the same mechanical movements, suddenly vanished on reaching the wall at the end of the corridor; nor did we, I am thankful to say see them again.

The SMELL had explained itself.

Anxious to get to Eunice and fearsome lest she should have fainted, I was about to quit the study, when my eyes were attracted to an object on the floor. It was the mysterious volume which, loosened from the shelf in some miraculous fashion, had fallen to the ground, and now lay open, its ponderous, gilded clasps undone and limp.

The fading sunlight concentrating its rays on the pages of the book in a final and prodigiously bloody effort, enabled me to read the following extract: "and for this great and unpardonable sin of the Abbess Hilda and the Monk Nicholas, we—the Saintly and Beloved Abbot Matthew, the learned Franciscan brother Raymond, the laymen and labourers, Barber and Brooks together with I, Sir John Hickson Leigh, Knight did entomb them alive, clasped in each other's arms, cursing man and blaspheming heaven, on the eve of the 11th day of August, 1521. And of the exact spot in the Abbey of Wolsey wherein they be buried, no man—save we who placed them there—knoweth, nor shall any discover the same until the day cometh when the secrets of all flesh shall be revealed."

This much I read and no more for the light proving too strong for me, I was compelled to remove my gaze and when I opened my eyes and saw again the volume it had gone, and lo! to my intense and unfeigned amazement it was back again in its customary place on the shelf, nor could the united efforts of myself and daughters remove it from that spot.

Regarding this extraordinary incident, as the only feasible explanation of the phenomena Eunice and I had seen, we could arrive at no other conclusion than that the house (once Wolsey Abbey) was haunted by the phantasms of the Abbess Hilda and the Monk Nicholas; and with such an explanation we have had to be content.

❑❑❑

NO. XYZ EUSTON ROAD

THE LITTLE OLD WOMAN IN THE HELIOTROPE SKIRT

Technical form of apparition: Phantasm of the dead
Source of authenticity: Personal experience of author
Cause of haunting: Murder

OF all the most annoying things in this world few are more so than missing one's train, especially when it happens to be the last in the day.

This unpleasant experience happened to me one evening early in September 1895. I came into Euston just as the 7 P.M. for Northampton—the last train connected with Brixworth—was steaming out of the station—and so, willy-nilly, I had to remain in town all night.

"Where to put up," now became the absorbing question. I wanted to be close to the station in order to catch the earliest morning train, but, although there were plenty of rich men's hotels, there seemed a sore dearth of "go-betweens;" it was either five shillings the night or sixpence; Purgatory or Hell: I could see no place that suited ME.

At last after traversing many squares and the more respectable of the side streets, I retraced my steps, eventually alighting on a private and inconsequential looking hotel in Euston Road.

The interior of the establishment was in keeping with the exterior—gloomy and forbidding, and the damp, earthy smell that seemed to rise from the basement made me gravely apprehensive of rheumatism; still the tariff was in strict accordance with my means, and feeling too tired to wander further, I decided to remain.

The room in which I had a very sparse supper was like the majority of dining-rooms in middle-class hotels: overcrowded with unwieldy furniture, frowsy, ill-ventilated; imagine that the table had been laid once and for all (it had undoubtedly presented the same spectacle for months), and that the cloth, never very white, was removed, only, when it grew too begrimed even for the blunted susceptibilities of the proprietress. I afterwards found that the beef did not belie its looks, that the bread was in excellent accord, and that the water might well have been the receptacle of innumerable generations of bacilli.

There were other visitors besides myself, either Germans or commercial travellers, probably both; but as their conversation carried on over plates of half raw meat, was neither particularly edifying nor interesting, I preferred an antique number of *Vanity Fair* until, at length, tiring of that, I picked up a candlestick and made my way to bed.

The moment I crossed the threshold of my room, that peculiar and indefinable sensation that invariably suggests the immediate proximity of the superphysical came over me, I felt sure the house was haunted. But by what? Ah! that was the problem left for ME to solve.

The furniture of the room was of the orthodox lodging-house type—inartistic, scant and seedy; a gaunt four-poster propped against the middle of the wall running at right angles to the door was adorned with exceedingly dirty valances of a nondescript pink and white pattern; facing this was a fireplace the register of which was of course down; to the left of this was a hanging wardrobe that I at once examined and found to contain nothing more formidable than a score or two of black-beetles that scuttled unceremoniously away into holes at the sight of my candle; whilst on the opposite side of the room, facing the window, was a rickety dressing-table surmounted by a still more rickety looking-glass. In one corner of the room stood a washing-stand from which the white paint had peeled in a hundred places, and in the other corner a dismantled bureau that resembled some vessel after a great storm. These, I believe, apart from a couple of cane-bottomed chairs, constituted the entire furniture, nor can I say this scantiness, taking into consideration the poorness of the quality, was any matter of regret.

The carpet, undoubtedly the best feature of the room, and either an Axminster or a Brussels—not being an expert on such a point I cannot tell which—hid all the boarding save where the margins were stained with a preparation of potash.

I give all these details to show that several years of practical investigation of haunted houses had developed my inquiring faculties to a very high degree, little, if anything, escaping my notice.

The *raison d'être* of ghosts often lies where it is least expected; in some article of furniture, not infrequently a cupboard near at hand, in the panelling, the skirting, or, not infrequently again, on or under the boards.

When I am in a haunted room, my first instinct, therefore, is to take a very careful stock of my surroundings; the bare appearance or touch of a piece of furniture often supplying me with the necessary clue.

On this occasion, however, nothing arousing my suspicions and feeling abnormally sleepy, I bolted my door and lay on the bed; I say "on," not "in," as a cursory glance at the pillow made me draw deductions as to the sheets. Within a few minutes I went to sleep, falling into a heavy, dreamless slumber from which I was suddenly and most alarmingly awakened by the feeling I was no longer alone in the room.

Opening my eyes, I perceived the apartment flooded with a bright unnatural light that apparently emanated from, or at all events accompanied, the figure of a little old woman with yellow hair and a heliotrope skirt. I noticed these idiosyncrasies of person and dress directly, the nature of the light accentuating them, and my senses being, as they always are in the presence of superphysical phenomena, wonderfully and painfully acute.

Standing in front of the dressing-table, the eccentric individual was examining herself with the greatest curiosity in the crazy looking-glass to which allusion has already been made.

Her profile was angular, her lack of colour ghastly, whilst from her ears hung that style of drop-earring worn by ladies in the days of the crinoline; otherwise her costume might have belonged to the latter seventies or early eighties. There was nothing actually HORRIBLE about her, save her reflection, and as my eyes turned with irresistible fascination towards the looking-glass, my blood turned to ice. The surface of the mirror, made preternaturally bright, flashed back the most hideous, the most incomparably HIDEOUS image of Fear.

Never! never in all my life had I seen depicted in aught but Wiertz's pictures such inconceivably awful terror as that which confronted me there—and now as I gazed at it, a sickly curiosity seized me as to what could be the origin of such Hellish Fear. Was it Fear of Death; of the Unknown metetherical Abysses; of Eternal Damnation; of what?

Then—as I followed the direction of the dilating pupils—I saw—God help me—the Cause! Descending from a few inches above her head were the snake-like coils of a rope. Had I been able to turn my head, maybe I should have seen whence they came; but I could not move a muscle, and could only feel the keynote to some great and hitherto unsolvable mystery was at hand but purposely hidden from me.

There was scant time for speculation. The enactment of this drama was brief as it was lurid; uttering an appalling scream that was quickly converted into a gurgle of the most blood-curdling significance, the old lady clawed the air with her spidery fingers.

The murderer was pitiless, the noose coming to with an irresistible snap, jerked the wretched victim off her feet.

For one instant—the most harrowing of all—I watched her falling backwards; watched the changing of her deadly pallor into a deep and vivid purple, watched the rolling of her starting eyeballs, the foam-flakes on her lips, and the frenzied movements of her stiffening arms and then—THEN—as she struck the ground with a reverberating crash—all was darkness. The ghostly tragedy for this night at least was over.

This I realised, but my nerves being too completely unstrung by what I had witnessed to allow me to sleep, I crept under the counterpane and lay there shivering till the welcome rays of early dawn converted the room into another place. My first movement was to examine the scene of the ghostly murder, and upon turning up the carpet, I discovered not a bloodstain, but a comparatively new piece of boarding!

With that, drawing my own conclusions, I had to rest content—there was nothing else in the room that could in any way have been transmuted into evidence.

The moment the clock struck six I picked up my valise, and gobbling down a lukewarm breakfast with little relish, quitted the house, determining to pay it another visit before very long.

In this, however, I was doomed to disappointment. Some months elapsed before I could again visit the neighbourhood of Euston, and when I did so, I found the hotel had vanished nor have I to this day been able to identify the house wherein I slept.

I have but lately been informed that a good many years ago (when we middle-aged fogies were mere children) a singularly repulsive murder was committed at a house in or near Euston Road, the victim being a somewhat extraordinary old lady. Further details I do not know, therefore I can only surmise that what I saw may possibly have been HER phantasm—but please remember, it is ONLY a surmise.

PANMAUR HOLLOW MERIONETH

THE BLACK PEDLAR

Technical form of apparition: Phantasm of the dead
Source of authenticity: "Ladies' Cabinet," 1835, and elsewhere
Cause of haunting: Murder

THE "Ladies Cabinet" for 1835 contains an account of a haunting in Merioneth that seems to me of sufficient psychic interest to record.

Hence I append it; but since the original text is a trifle too intricate in places, I have taken the liberty to tell the story more or less in my own words:

"In the summer of 1832 I was on a walking tour in Wales; in selecting, as the principal scene of my operations, Merioneth, and chancing one evening to be overtaken by a storm, when midway between Dolgelly and Bala, I was speedily placed in the most unpleasant of predicaments. To go on I was afraid, to turn back was impossible; what could I do? The night was dark, the rain almost tropical, and the roadway so broken up with furrows that I could only grope along with the utmost difficulty; whilst the frequent windings, steep ascents, and sharp declivities not only added to my embarrassment, but greatly increased my weariness. At every few yards I either plunged into a miniature morass or, stumbling over a boulder, found myself smarting in the centre of a gorse bush.

"At length I grew desperate—human nature could stand it no longer—and resolving to perish with the cold rather than flounder on under such pitiable conditions, I threw myself down on a rock and prepared to lie there till daybreak.

"It is possible I had remained in this position for ten or so minutes, when I was roused to a sense of deliverance by the bright glow of a lamp, and starting up to my feet, I discovered I was no longer alone.

Confronting me was the figure of a short man, wrapped in a shaggy great-coat, and wearing a slouched hat. He was holding a lantern in his hand. By a series of pantomimic gestures he assured me that his intentions were amicable, and that he was anxious to guide me to some place of shelter where I should have a more comfortable pallet than a bare rock.

"I accepted his offer, though not without some misgivings, as I could not remember ever having met with any one quite so uncouth or bizarre.

"Turning abruptly to the right he struck across a wide moor covered with gorse and innumerable boulders, and so studded with pools of water that I seemed to be in a perpetual state of wading. Emerging from this, we wended our way along the side of a precipice, at the bottom of which roared one of those mountain torrents so characteristic of all parts of Wales.

"Beckoning to me to follow, my guide mysteriously disappeared, and peering over the edge of the chasm, I perceived him, to my amazement, making his descent by an almost invisible and perpendicular pathway. For a second or so I hesitated, and then, making up my mind to brave anything rather than remain by myself in such an unfamiliar and dangerous neighbourhood, I gingerly lowered myself over the brink, and, after a few tumbles, succeeded in overtaking him just as he arrived at the bottom.

"We now found ourselves in a valley of stygian darkness, and of such restricted dimensions that the spray from the river bathed me from head to foot. My companion pressed resolutely on, and, maintaining the same extraordinary and uncanny silence, conducted me to a recess in the hillside where the outlines of a bare, dismantled house gradually arose to greet us. It was merely a pile of ruins, old, yet naked, without any of those evidences of vegetation one usually associates with the antique. I particularly noticed this deficiency; it impressed and perplexed me. If moss and lichens grew elsewhere—why not here?

"The situation of the house was strikingly romantic and weird—indeed, one could not well imagine a more dismal spot. A giant mass of black rock reared itself in the background like a Brobdingnagian bat. In the foreground, and at so close a distance that the spray blowing madly over my face and clothes drenched me to the skin, rushed a seething mass of sable water, whilst to accentuate all this Avernian horror, the wind whistled demoniacally, and the rain fell with ever-increasing fury. Turning to my guide, I impatiently requested him 'to move on,' and take me with the greatest expedition to the nearest available hostelry.

"In reply he took off his hat, and, thrusting his monstrous head forward, revealed to my horror-stricken gaze a shapeless, sodden mass of black flesh!

"The cause of his silence was now obvious—he couldn't speak because he had no mouth; but neither had he eyes, ears, or nose; nothing but that awful, unmeaning, rotund protuberance.

"I stood aghast, too terrified to stir, almost too terrified to breathe, with the hideous Thing looming there before me, and the booming of the river behind. It was a ghastly situation.

"The creature advanced an inch—my blood turned to ice; it raised its arms—my soul sickened within me; it lunged suddenly forward—and—fell right through me. As it did so I heard a fiendish chuckle, which, dying slowly out, gave way to a succession of blood-curdling groans that seemed to proceed from the interior of the ruins. The figure, however, was nowhere to be seen; it must have dematerialised on the spot.

"Very much relieved at this, though still considerably frightened, I was now able to use my limbs, and turning my back on the ghostly building, I felt my way along the bank of the river. I dare not glance at the boiling foam, the very sound of it made my flesh creep; nor did

I feel in any degree safe till a winding of the footpath brought me to a bridge, on the opposite side of which I saw the twinkling lights of many houses. I was now, once again, in the land of the living, and a substantial meal by a cosy fire helped, in a good measure, to dissipate my fears and recompense me for all the trials I had undergone.

"Prior to leaving the inn next day I learned from my host that the hollow was known to be haunted, and, on that account, was universally shunned after sunset. Half a century ago the ruins—then a neat grey cottage—had been inhabited by the Evanses, a bad, thriftless 'lot.'

"At the instigation of her husband, and with the motive of robbery, Mrs. Evans, a buxom woman—handsome in a bad bold style—had flirted openly with a pedlar, known locally as 'Black Dave.'

"This man was easily induced to put up at their house, and his suspicions being lulled to rest by the amorous overtures of the woman, he was surprised in his sleep and butchered.

"Fearing, however, either to commit the body to the river or bury it in their garden lest it should be found, and being at the time very hard pressed for food—they improvised an oven in the earth and ate it!

"The vengeance of Heaven was, however, close on their track; the cottage, paid for out of their ill-gotten gains, caught fire during a drunken carousal, and Mrs. Evans was burned to death, whilst her husband only lingered long enough to make a full confession of the crime.

"The house was never rebuilt; the phantasm of Dave, in the disgusting guise in which he appeared to me, still haunts the precincts, and, delighting to gull unsuspecting wayfarers, leads them out of their proper courses, guiding them with a fiendish skill to the black ruin—the scene of his ghastly murder."

❑❑❑

CATCHFIELD HALL, THE MIDLANDS

THE TERRIBLE HEADS THAT RISE THROUGH THE FLOOR

Technical form of apparitions: Phantoms of the dead

Source of authenticity: Accumulative hearsay evidence

No. — THE TERRACE, WORCESTER.

March 1, 1908.

DEAR MR. ELLIOTT O'DONNELL,

I thought you would be interested to hear I met Mrs. Blake last night at the Stowes, where I got out of her with no small amount of pumping an account of "what she saw" at that notorious ball at Catchfield some years ago. It is very horrible, too horrible, perhaps even for such a "spook gourmand" as you. Of course all the names I have given you are fictitious. You know there have been several libel cases lately, in connection with haunted houses so that one cannot be too careful. &c. &c. &c.

Yours sincerely,
EVELYN D. O'GRADY.

THE STORY

My invitation to spend the Christmas holidays with Lady Wentworth came as a delightful surprise.

Imagine me a poor, insignificant little schoolmistress in St. Rudolphs, suddenly blossoming out into a much envied guest at Catchfield. Who can blame me if I indulged in a momentary outburst of pride?

So far my lot in life had not been all *couleur de rose*. Losing my husband shortly after our marriage, I had been obliged to do something for a bare living.

My education though fair had fallen short of Girton or a degree, and I was barely qualified to teach any but very small children. Had I but foreseen the future, I might no doubt have done better. As it was my position was only that of a kindergarten schoolmistress in St. Rudolphs.

I do not think you can truly estimate a person's disposition till you see how they behave to those who have the misfortune to be in subordinate positions, nor can you always tell a shoddy lady from a real one until you have discovered how she treats her governess and servants. Until I taught in St. Rudolphs I had no idea how thoroughly common were the majority of its so-called aristocracy, but one term was quite sufficient to show me that dealing with such hopelessly and innately vulgar people would be almost more than I could bear.

It was therefore scarcely a matter of wonder—that when Christmas drew nigh—the Christmas after my first sojourn in St. Rudolphs—I was almost beside myself with joy on receiving a pressing invitation to stay at Catchfield Hall. Nothing soothes the sensitive nature of a snob more than to call other people snobbish. The parents of my children were of the middle class—middlish—snobs with a very big S, and should any one need a proof of the correctness of this assertion let me point to him the fact that whenever a moneyed person came to reside within any get-at-able distance whatever, the people I have designated as "snobs" made all haste to call on them; even the bishop whose object in coming to St. Rudolphs was obviously only "to confirm," was inundated with invitations to dinner, and the rival claims to eligibility of those invited to meet him, were openly discussed at afternoon tea and bridge parties. Let me also add that their club, ludicrously labelled "select," boycotted one of its members for some trivial remark, true enough, but like so many other homely truths better left unsaid, and that these very people who had sat in judgment, themselves indulged in the most scathingly rude remarks to those who for certain reasons were obliged to "grin and bear it."

Therefore I repeat again, the parents of my children were snobs, and being snobs would not allow any one in the humble position of a schoolmistress to say any thing that might in any way be construed into snobbishness.

Depict to yourself then how indignant they were, and how I laughed up my sleeve when I let slip, quite by mischance you understand, the fact that I was going to spend Christmas with my near, my very near kinsman Lord Robert Wentworth.

A schoolmistress related to a peer! How preposterous! how absurd! how snobbish! and they laughed at first scornfully, then incredulously—then pityingly, and I—I humbly bowed them out of the house, and running upstairs continued my packing. Vale St. Rudolphs! Welcome Catchfield!

Under these circumstances you can imagine why I tell you all this—it is to show you how more than overjoyed I was at the thought of eating my Christmas pudding among gentlefolk.

When I got out at Highfield—the nearest station to Catchfield—my lord's brougham stood in waiting.

"They are very full up at the Hall, madam," the coachman said, touching his hat respectfully, "otherwise miladi would have sent one of the motors, but they have both had to go out longish distances."

"Is there a house-party?" I faltered, giving one of the horses—I love horses—a gentle pat on the head.

"What! didn't you know? I beg your pardon, madam," the fellow added suddenly, recollecting himself, "but it is the Coming of Age party of the Hon. Walter early next week that has fetched well-nigh half the county; you see he is the eldest son—and—well, madam, there is to be a very big ball. I made sure madam knew all about it."

I shook my head despairingly, balls were not for such as I. I had neither a dress nor yet the money wherewith to buy one. Most decidedly I ought not to have come! I glanced at the man to see if he understood my misgivings, apparently he did not; perhaps he would not; his manner at all events was in no degree less deferential, and as he shut the carriage door with the courtly air of an old gallant, I compared him with the parents at St. Rudolphs—the comparison of course being all in his favour.

I will not attempt to describe the exterior of Catchfield, it has been done so often and so well in historical romances, in biographies, and in County Directories that any additional effort of mine would be at once superfluous and poor.

I arrived there late—too late for dinner—and partook of a dainty supper laid expressly for me in the ball-room presumptive. Fancy supper by myself in a ball-room! But there was apparently a doubt as to which of the rooms would be used for the occasion, his lordship being somewhat reluctant at present to allow this handsomely, I might almost say sombrely, furnished apartment to be used for such a frivolous purpose.

Remembering Robert's sanctimonious bringing up I was not in the least surprised at his qualms, my only wonder being that he countenanced a ball at all, but of course that was miladi's doings. I much wished to inquire why a solitary meal for such as I should be served in a room of such splendid dimensions, and one that in most households would undoubtedly have been used as a drawing-room, but I refrained, not desiring to appear inquisitive in the eyes of the servants. Her ladyship arrived as I was finishing my second cup of fragrant coffee, and despite a certain languid hauteur characteristic of the nobility, especially of the MODERN nobility, she appeared to welcome me.

I felt this, and yet somehow I was puzzled—puzzled at an indescribable something in her manner that was quite apart from pride—something that left me with the decidedly unpleasant impression she was surely acting a part, and—yet—why should she? Why should her ladyship be anything but frank with the poor and inoffensive cousin of her husband?

But what was it that made her eyes fall as they encountered mine, and wander furtively round the room; and why that sudden look of fear that crept into them as they alighted on the fireplace.

"You wont mind sitting here till bedtime, will you?" she observed, "I will tell Webster, my maid, to bring you your candle at eleven o'clock. If there is anything you want, you have only to tell HER. All our guests play bridge, and I concluded from what Robert told me you didn't approve of gambling, so I thought you would be happier here. We are expecting other anti-gamblers in a few days, so your banishment will only be temporary! You will excuse us for a time, wont you?"

What other reply could I give but "O yes! most certainly! It is indeed kind of you to allow me the use of such a lovely room, &c.," and Lady Wentworth departed from my presence with a gracious—a most patronising and highly gracious smile. I was of course charmed and flattered, as any poor connection by marriage should be, but I wished all the same that Robert had also come to welcome me, I should have felt more at ease with Robert! I liked Robert, and—well, I did not like his beautiful and accomplished wife. Had he come only for two minutes I should not have minded, but I was tired, I felt neglected, and I longed for kindness. Kindness after St. Rudolphs. It was not like Robert, we had been such friends in our youth; children together, playmates, chums! Had money and position changed his nature?

Money! I grew dispirited! I was poor! terribly poor! I was lonely! Oh, so lonely!

The room was huge, the night cold and the fire SMALL—very small.

Drawing my chair close to it I simulated ease; I tried to feel cosy! Cosy!

What a barrier, an insurmountable barrier, was poverty to pleasure! Would Robert's wife have banished a countess? Fancy a countess experiencing a reception such as this! A countess in a vast room empty save for draughts and a Liliputian fire! A countess! I laughed! I was growing common like the mediocre parents of St. Rudolphs. Vulgarity is catching! It is both epidemic and endemic.

Had Robert told her I disapproved of playing cards for money? Of course not, that was a society taradiddle! He couldn't know my scruples or he would never have asked me to meet his wife. She, she had guessed my poverty by my profession—all schoolmistresses are poor; every one that teaches is poor—education must be gratis. A cold blast of air from the chimney made me shiver. The room was indeed draughty! and how still! I did not altogether like such stillness, it got on my nerves. And how dark! Why were not all the gas jets lighted—why only this one? Because I was poor; the poor should learn to be economical, and example is better than precept! Hence this feeble flicker: a flicker that failing to reach the further extremities of the chamber, left the corners enveloped in shrouds of darkness—of a black impenetrable darkness I could neither fathom nor comprehend. The furniture was superb, but it was of too funereal a texture and colour to be pleasing to me just then, I would have preferred something of a brighter tone.

The floor was covered by a carpet that must assuredly have been made expressly for that room since it stretched right up to the skirting, concealing every particle of bare board.

I could not see the pattern, I could only devise by the soft tread of the carpet that it was either of Persian or Turkish manufacture. In some places, where kissed by the moonlight, it was almost white, whilst in other parts it was rendered black by a hotch-potch of countless shadows lying thick upon it.

Through the great bay windows opposite me, a magnificent panorama of lawn, meadows and rivers, beyond which I fancied I could detect the needle-like front of a steeple, spread itself before my eyes. All this natural beauty lay enhanced by a thin covering of gleaming snow. It was Christmas! The glamour of the hour and season enchanted me; past injuries and St. Rudolphs were forgotten; I was at peace with all men.

At peace! What wouldn't I give if I could always be so; if these broad acres, this noble mansion, this stately apartment were mine—mine—ALL MINE—and the stillness of the room again oppressed me.

Where were the many guests miladi had mentioned? Where were the sounds of revelry? The high-pitched voices of women, the hoarser tones of men, the indistinct murmuring of conversation such as I had sat and listened to in days of yore; how it had hummed and buzzed around me when plunged in pleasant reverie, it then had no more effect on my hearing than the lapping of the gentlest waves on the seashore. There were no such sounds now; these massive walls were a sure, impenetrable barrier to whatever might be going on outside—this room—far from being filled with giddy babblers—was empty, distractedly, painfully EMPTY, empty save for the dancing moonbeams and the moving shadows.

But was it empty? My heart gave a violent, sickly throb as I recollected the look of disquietude, of grave, of indisputably grave apprehension in miladi's eyes as she peered around! Of what had she been afraid—of the approaching twilight, of the shadows, of the gloom; and as I cast a terrified glance ahead of me I fancied—foolish fancy! that those palls of darkness I have already mentioned had come out further from the nooks and crannies and were fast approaching me.

Those of us who have ever ridden on horseback by night across some dreary wilderness, or along a lonely road have doubtless had occasion to observe a strange alteration in the behaviour of our beast; its psychic propensities have been suddenly and mysteriously awakened; it fights shy of some particular tree, or stone, or gap in the hedge; its ears twitch, its flanks quiver, it is all on the tremble, the slightest sound would now make it take the bit between its teeth and bolt; it is afraid not necessarily of what it has seen, but what it fears may be there! And—to an anomalous species of terror I found myself a bounden slave.

I dreaded to think of the effect even the most trivial sound or incident might now produce on my agitated mind. Had I been able, I would have risked the displeasure of my hostess and left the room, but I COULD NOT; every atom of strength seemed to have quitted my body—I was *pro tempore* cataleptic—PARALYSED.

A faint and almost imperceptible movement suddenly attracted my attention to a square patch of light on the carpet immediately before me.

To my horror something was coming THROUGH the floor. Slowly, very slowly, first of all a head, a head surmounted with long dishevelled black hair, then a FACE! God save me from seeing the like again—a face that might have once been beautiful, or plain, or ugly, but was now—NOTHING—nothing—I won't describe—nothing but the GRAVE; then shoulders, bust, what was once a body, legs. Held in its arms in close embrace—was the figure of a baby—in a like state of nudity and decay.

For a moment, only for a moment, they stood swaying silently to and fro in the moonlight, and then with a snakelike movement of her body the phantom of the woman glided across the room, vanishing in the recess containing the large bay window.

After the subsidation of intense terror at this hideous spectacle I had been compelled to witness, the pulsating of my heart once again becoming normal, I was able to reflect with comparative calmness on what I had seen.

I say with comparative calmness, for a strong suspicion now entered my mind that Lady Wentworth may have anticipated all along what would happen, and that I had been put in that room as a mere experiment to see whether it were still haunted. The bare idea of such perfidy filled me with so great an indignation that I seriously thought of trumping up some excuse and returning home; my resolutions being shattered only by the opportune arrival of Cousin Robert, whose cordial welcome acting like a stimulant made me decide to remain.

With a thoughtfulness that had singled him out from among his companions as a boy, he noticed my weariness, and putting it down to the fatigue of my journey went in search of his wife's maid.

Need I say that I was thankful to get to bed and there, despite my ghostly adventures, I slept very soundly till the gong went for breakfast, at which free and easy meal I made the acquaintance of some very charming guests.

Miladi was of course too much in request to spend more than a few minutes with poor, insignificant me; she expressed an earnest hope that I had not been too dull for words and that I had found the room warm and comfortable. "At all events," she added, "you can sit and read there without fear of interruption. I know how fond of books you 'clever' people are—you must go into the library and choose some. You were not disturbed last night were you?"

Though this question was put in the most artless manner possible and with all apparent ingenuousness I detected a half frightened, half inquiring expression in her eyes that she vainly tried to stifle, an expression which converted the suspicion I had entertained into a conviction, a conviction that this woman was isolating me to serve some deep and subtle purpose.

I tried to get out of the lady's-maid what this purpose might be, but if Webster knew she most certainly showed no signs of it, being doubtless as accomplished an actress as her mistress.

As one may readily conclude I looked forward to the evening with little equanimity, offering up fervent prayers for any incident that might add to the duration of dinner.

Now I hate grand dinners as a rule; their regality unnerves me; I am appalled at the number of people; at the dazzling display of plate, at the multiplicity of the courses (many of the dishes being unknown to me), at the ceaseless flow of conversation, at the clatter of glasses, at the wine, at everything; but on this occasion I simply revelled in it; the greatest formalities appealed to me as pleasantly distracting; I was poor, my companions wealthy scions of the aristocracy. I had nothing to do but eat—eat and be silent; be silent and listen; listen and look, and I saw all that one would have wanted to see in the atelier of the very best costumière in Paris or the West End.

My own dress was shabby but what of that! No one seemed aware of it, no one noticed me; I was a nonentity, mute, a consuming machine; in no one's way because each of my neighbours was far too engrossed in eating to care about carrying on a conversation.

Once I thought a lady cast a half enviable glance at my hands; they are my best point, particularly so, when nicely manicured—and once I imagined, dear Robert, but there, THAT was only imagination.

Well the dinner, like all good things, came to an end at last. I enjoyed the dessert most; the bonbons were heavenly; every one ate them as if they were hungry; I caught myself actually pitying our hostess. At a signal from miladi, we all got up; I left the other ladies in the hall; they trooped away to fetch their purses, whilst I, feeling very much like some poor whipped schoolgirl, slunk off to the ball-room.

It was not until the door closed behind me, I understood the full horror of the situation; I was alone! for the second time within twenty-four hours—in that chamber—Alone! Alone save for those foul pollutions that might rise at any instant from beneath the floor. I believe, even then, I would have flown had not the stubbornness and pride innate in all my family restrained me. Come what would, her ladyship should never call me a coward.

So—I stuck to my post with heroic resolutions. Much as I suffered the previous day, my sufferings then in comparison with now were small, nor did the dreadful anticipations that tortured me without cessation as I sat there, waiting for the boards to part asunder, in any way surpass the awful realisation. Step by step, detail by detail the psychic drama was repeated in all its damnable horror; my recovery after witnessing it being slower on this occasion, accompanied by relapses into a state of terror too painful even to recall.

Yet I survived and succeeded in so far pulling myself together, that I met the kindly greeting of her ladyship at breakfast next morning with a calm and unembarrassed air. She did not suspect me. Once again the ordeal came and miladi, with a refinement of cruelty worthy of her steel-blue eyes and thin lips, herself conducted me to the fatal ball-room.

"To-morrow, you will have company," she murmured, her face shining white amid that semi-gloom, "I must apologise for not giving you more light, but—for some UNEARTHLY reason or other—only one of those gas jets will ever burn. Odd is it not?" And as her eyes met mine, I walked to the fire and burst out laughing.

She was disarmed! Could any one laugh who was afraid of ghosts?

She speedily, VERY speedily left me and once again I underwent it ALL.

Suspense—horror—prostration. I think I suffered more this third night than on either of the other two.

Yet, long before morning I had recovered from the shock.

I saw a look of genuine relief rush into her ladyship's face as she encountered my smiling countenance: whatever apprehensions she might have had with regard to THAT room were now unquestionably removed.

"It must be cleared out without further delay!" I heard her remark to Robert, "the floor will take some time polishing—and—remember the incandescent burners!"

The incandescent burners! I chuckled, what effect would THEY have on GHOSTS. I half expected she would now tell me why she had been anxious I should remain in the room: she was assured it was no longer haunted, why trouble about the past?

But a moment's reflection made me think that after all it might be "the past" she was most anxious to conceal; hauntings, especially of so gruesome a nature as this, usually point to some blot on the escutcheon, to a disreputable something in the history of the house—and that is why so many people object to seeing their family ghosts appear in print.

Accordingly, miladi, having the honour of the Wentworths at heart, would take very good care she did not give me as much as a hint as to what she herself, quite possibly, attributed to legends.

Webster did indeed favour me with the information, that neither her ladyship nor any one else, save Lord Wentworth and the old charwoman (who dusted) were ever known to enter the room, at all events since SHE had been at the Hall, and that was well nigh ten years; which information clearly implied that entrance was strictly forbidden.

It was interesting to speculate what course miladi would have adopted, had I told her what I had seen! She was proud, domineering and tactful; would she have "pooh-poohed!" the whole thing; commanded me to be silent; resorted to bribery, or what? I couldn't imagine her pleading—and yet—the Honour of the Old Aristocracy is very dear to them; they sometimes value it more than—life.

• • • •

THE NEXT FEW DAYS PASSED agreeably and all too quickly for me. The non-card playing element, though rather stiff and prudish, were kindly disposed towards me, no doubt on account of my shy disposition and impecunious widowhood.

Of Robert I saw very little; the host and hostess in a big house never have a moment to spare. To prepare the ball-room an extra staff of servants was employed incessantly for three days, at the end of which time it was pronounced ready for the occasion.

I can find no words to convey to others the singular way in which the altered room impressed me. Though stripped of all its massive, gloomy furniture, brilliantly illuminated with many jets of incandescent gas (Robert had a strange aversion to electricity) and adorned with festoons of Oriental flowers, banners, and the gayest coloured bunting, it still retained an air of sadness, and an indescribable something, that nothing, nothing short of total annihilation, could ever eradicate or modify.

Her ladyship clad in a snowy dress of the most costly material trimmed with the rarest lace, her fair arms and bosom glittering with the Wentworth diamonds, looked like a fairy queen standing on the threshold of an enchanted castle.

I looked closely at her but could see no remnant of apprehension either in her eyes or gestures, she was perfectly at ease and sublimely unconscious of aught but the enjoyment of those around her and the importance attached to herself, the well-dressed handsome hostess.

With Robert it was otherwise; in spite of his smiles, his bows, his many pretty actions of old-world gallantry, I could see that the wan, grey spirit of unrest stalking at his elbow never left him. He would have staked his soul to glance occasionally at the spot before the fireplace, but fear lest some one might see him effectually held him back. This continual mental struggle, unsuspected even by his wife, was only too obviously apparent to me, and I seemed to hear a sigh of relief—of deep and earnest relief—issue from his lips when the orchestra began.

And now all was symphony and movement. There was much glare and glitter and piquancy; snake-like evolutions, spasmodic convergences, dexterous extrications, all performed and repeated with mathematical precision and untiring repetition.

The music changed—the waltz gave place to a novel and somewhat wildly executed fandango. It was her ladyship's whim to include in her programme exotic dances; a resuscitation of long-forgotten Terpsichore, they were undoubtedly the distinguishing and characteristic features of her entertainments, raising them far above the commonplace, and gaining for miladi a world-wide and much-coveted reputation. She hated anything merely popular and vulgar.

In this dance that now commenced and which I beheld for the first time, there was much of the beautiful, the wanton, the *bizarre*, and just a suspicion of "something" which might have shocked a very exacting "Grundy."

As the greater number of the guests, like myself, were unacquainted with it, the floor was left comparatively free for the performers, the onlookers lining the walls, the doorway, and the big bay window.

Never had I witnessed such enthusiasm; the dancers, throwing their very heart and soul into their antics, gyrated and pirouetted in such lively fashion as evoked spontaneous outbursts of applause from the delighted, albeit bewildered and somewhat puzzled spectators.

The faster the music, the quicker the feet, the louder the clapping.

And now, at a moment when the revelry had reached its height and the attention of all was riveted on the dancers, a sudden commotion in their midst made everybody wonder. What was it? What had happened?

I glanced at the clock, Robert glanced too; our eyes met, and I read in his a deadly fear; it was the hour for the dead to rise.

The space in front of the fireplace was now deserted, and the dancers, grouped around on either side, were eagerly peering forward to ascertain the cause of their alarm.

Curiosity, repulsion, and horror—horror wild and undiluted—were now depicted on every countenance as the gently heaving boards, slipping noiselessly asunder, revealed two hideous heads, rising as it were from the bowels of the earth.

Slowly, very slowly, with a gradation suggestive of machinery, the phantoms I knew so well at length came into full view. But stupendous as was the sensation this unlooked-for tableau produced, not a sound was uttered—and, as if to accentuate the silence, the music broke off abruptly, dancers, audience, and orchestra being similarly affected.

For a few seconds the female phantom, clutching in one arm its loathsome burden, paused irresolutely beside its tomb—and then, shaking a hand in the direction of the Honourable Walter, it made a sudden dart at the spot where he stood.

A thrill of the most intense horror accompanied this unexpected movement, all eyes being now transferred to the wretched youth.

I gave one glance at my cousin Robert—I dare not look again—his expression was frightful—he could do nothing to help his son—his position was that of the damned.

The crucial moment arrived—no one breathed—the Things from the Grave reached Walter—there was no hesitation—they passed RIGHT THROUGH him. I looked at the wall, I rubbed my eyes—the spectres had vanished!

A convulsive throb now ran through the assemblage, the revellers exchanged frightened and embarrassed glances, there was a general movement to the door, the room emptied, the dance was over.

• • • •

I DID NOT SEE HER LADYSHIP again—I merely received a message of farewell, but Robert came to say good-bye.

"I wonder," he said, gazing at me with his pensive harrowed eyes, "I wonder very much if the ghosts appeared to you when alone in that room? If so you have indeed been brave, and to keep it secret served us right. The story of the hauntings," he continued, "has up to the present been revealed only to the male members of our family, but to you I feel that an explanation is due. At any rate, you are a Wentworth and have given me ample proof that you may with safety be entrusted with a secret.

"It seems years ago that one of my ancestors got entangled in some way or another with a beautiful gipsy. She begged him to marry her; he refused; and fearful lest the affair should leak out and so bring discredit upon the family, he murdered her, burying her body, together with that of her child, underneath the ballroom floor. At least so the MS. states, and no one, as far as I am aware, has ever disproved it.

"Tortured with remorse and a victim to the orthodox fears of a murderer, my unhappy forefather took poison, commanding in his will 'that the ballroom should never again be used for a frivolous purpose,' an injunction which, until last night, has been faithfully obeyed.

"The Wentworths, as you may naturally suppose, have kept the story strictly to themselves—the male heirs alone being usually acquainted with it.

"I did not altogether credit the story of the haunting though my father swore he had seen the cursed apparitions. Moreover he told me that they appeared periodically—every night at 11 P.M. from the 20th to the 31st of December. He also warned me, and here I am much to blame, on no account to permit any outsider to be in the room, 'for if you do,' he added, 'THEN, something terrible will happen.' I own I was sceptical and bitterly I regret it now. I had never seen an apparition, and what my father told me he had seen, I attributed to Suggestion, the natural consequence of dwelling too much on the horrible details of the story.

"Maud shared my scepticism and when she wanted to use the room, brought forward the most ingenious arguments to overcome my scruples.

"I declared it was impossible—it would be sheer sacrilege. I was accused of inconsistency. I disbelieved! how then could there be any danger!—the injunction in the will was unreasonable and absurd. In short, I had no peace, I had to yield, so making the stipulation that we should first find out some means by which we could prove that there was no foundation for the story of the haunting, I reluctantly gave my consent.

"Somewhat to my astonishment, Maud had already formed a plan for testing the room. She had heard me speak of you, you were a Wentworth; if you discovered anything we could rely on you to keep it secret—and so my wife suggested that you should be put in the room, 'just to sample it.' I hesitated, I did not speak. I suppose my silence gave consent: the rest you know. I won't press you to tell me if you saw those beastly things, if you did the sequel only serves us right. Anyhow nothing can excuse my having sanctioned disobedience to that injunction in the will.

"The fact and the nature of the haunting is a secret no longer—the cause none but a Wentworth shall ever know.

"I need hardly enjoin you who are one of us to maintain silence on that point.

"We shall shut up the house for a time, until, in fact, the worst of the affair has blown over—and—when we meet again, let us hope it will be under happier circumstances."

We never met again; within six months of my departure, both Robert and his son were dead—killed in a motor accident abroad. The property is now in the hands of distant, of VERY distant relations, and I feel no compunction in saying what I know about it.

Only—if you repeat this to Mr. Elliott O'Donnell, please substitute fictitious names.

BURLE FARM, NORTH DEVON

THE HEADLESS DOG AND THE EVIL TREE

Technical form of apparitions: Elemental
Source of authenticity: First-hand evidence
Cause of hauntings: Unknown

BETWEEN my exit from the stage in 1900 up till quite recently I had the great, the very great misfortune to be a teacher in a small town in the north of England.

I say misfortune because I found the contrasts between exciting stageland and the monotonous schoolroom, between the generous and jovial theatrical fraternity and the mean and petty local parents, too decidedly pronounced to be other than excessively unpleasant.

I had small patience with the mediocre abilities of very mediocre children, and still less with the continual and unwarrantable interference of their ill-mannered and doting mothers. No lot in life could have been more thoroughly uncongenial than mine; indeed, it would have soon become unbearable had it not been for the constant influx of strangers whose presence in the town made an oasis in the desert.

It is to one of these visitors—Miss Medley—that I owe the following story.

"Some years ago," she began, "I received an invitation to spend August with a very crochety old aunt of mine residing at Burle Farm, North Devon.

"There was nothing at all extraordinary in the appearance of the house; it belonged to a type common in all parts of England. It was a low, rambling building of yellow stone with a good, substantial, thatched roof and ample stabling. The rooms, sweet with the scent of jasmine and honeysuckle, compared more than favourably with the stuffy dens in which I had been obliged to live in London; whilst the diamond-shaped window-panes and massive oak beams serving as supports to the ceilings, struck me as being quite delightfully quaint.

"My aunt, too—a rosy-faced old lady in a mob-cap—appeared quite in harmony with her surroundings. She was kindness itself—indeed, no one could have made me feel more thoroughly at home.

"'Folks do say the house is haunted,' she laughed, 'particularly one room—but there! I have never seen anything, and I don't suppose you will.'

"'A ghost!' I cried, 'how awfully exciting! oh! do let me sleep in the haunted room,' and I continued to plead till the kind-hearted old lady reluctantly consented.

"'You mustn't blame me if the ghost should visit you, Rosie,' she said; 'remember I have warned you.'

"'There is nothing I should enjoy better than seeing a real *bona-fide* spook, auntie dear,' I rejoined, smiling; but my aunt shook her head reprovingly, and no more was said on the subject until the next day.

"I awoke that night as the clock struck two—indeed, I fancied my awakening was due to that striking, it seemed so unusually loud and emphatic.

"It was a fine—indeed, I might say glorious—night, for although there was no moon, the heavens were so brilliantly illuminated with myriads of scintillating stars, that I could see every object around me almost as clearly as if it had been day.

"A sudden movement near the foot of the bed made me recollect my aunt's admonition. I listened, experiencing none of those pleasant anticipations of which I had spoken so boastfully.

"I knew no one could have entered the room, as I had taken the precaution to lock the door, having first of all looked under the bed and made a thorough examination of the hanging wardrobe. Consequently my visitor, unless a mouse or a rat, could be nothing material.

"I devoutly wished I had slept in one of the other rooms.

"A faint and sickly odour now became perceptible whilst the noise hitherto uninterpretable developed into a series of unequal knocks just as if some big animal were lying on the floor 'scratching' itself.

"Determined not to appear frightened I put my hand out of bed and called 'Trot! Trot! is that you?' (Trot being the name of my auntie's retriever.)

"Something instantly jumped up and, coming round the bed, stood by my side. Wondering whether it could be Trot, though at a loss to understand how he could have got into the room without being seen, I stretched out my fingers and to my intense relief touched a furry coat—the stench at the same time becoming so truly awful that I retched.

"I could, of course have satisfied myself as to the identity of my visitor by merely looking, but this, I am ashamed to say, I was too great a coward to do; a strange feeling telling me that I was in the presence of something unnatural.

"Running my hand fearfully along the shaggy skin of the animal, I felt for its head, discovering to my intense horror that it had none, the neck terminating in a wet mass of something soft and spongy.

"Unable to restrain myself any longer, I now looked, perceiving to my infinite terror a huge shock-haired spaniel, headless, and in the most abominable state of decomposition.

"I gazed at it for some seconds too appalled either to stir or utter a sound—this paralytic condition continuing till an abortive effort of the phantasm to jump on the bed loosened my tongue and I shrieked for help.

"The dog immediately vanished.

"My feelings had been, however, so outraged by what I had witnessed that nothing would have induced me to pass the remainder of the night in that room—my own idea was to get out of it with the utmost celerity.

"I did so—nor did I ever again—not even by daylight—venture to cross its threshold.

"My aunt, poor dear, was very much upset at the occurrence.

"She could not imagine how it was other people could see the ghost while she could not. And her scepticism was but natural; she was unable to grasp the idea that the psychic faculty is a gift, only granted to the few, and as rare as that either of music or painting.

"Other reasons for her incredulity in this particular occult manifestation lay in the enigmatical nature and purport of the phenomenon.

"In what category of ghosts would one classify a headless dog; Was it the spirit of a dog that had been decapitated on earth?

"She had never gathered from the Scriptures that beasts had souls—what then was this phantom of a dog?

"I suggested it might be a Poltergeist or Elemental, one of those purely bestial creations that for various reasons which you explained at your recent lecture—always haunt certain localities?"

"Yes!" I said, interrupting Miss Medley, "the sub-animal type of elemental is fairly common—if you refer to the June number 1908 of the magazine published by the Society for Psychical Research you will see an extremely well authenticated case of the haunting of a village by a white pig with an abnormally long snout and I could enumerate many other similar instances. But continue!"

"My aunt," Miss Medley went on, "informed me that the house had once been occupied by a lady who had lived a very selfish—not to say sensual life. She had settled down at Burle, after having been divorced twice, and her weekly routine was one incessant whirl of pleasure.

"She died without the consolation of the Church, surrounded by a crowd of fawning money-hunters and over-gorged poodles, so that for this, as well as other reasons I think there may be an alternative solution to the haunting. Is it not possible that what I saw was actually the spirit of this worldly woman, which thoroughly brutalised by long indulgence in sensuality had gradually adapted that shape most befitting IT."

"And the moral of that, Miss Medley," I observed, "is—if you do not wish to become a beast do not live like one! Yes! there is much to be learned from a study of the different types of phantasms—more I believe than from any pulpit discourses. Is that your only psychic experience?"

Miss Medley shook her head. "No!" she said, "I had another very gruesome one at Burle. After the dog episode my aunt thought fit to warn me not to pass along a certain road after dusk. 'There is an elm standing close to it,' she said, 'which the people about here declare to be haunted; as you have seen one ghost you may see another—so please be careful!'

"Now you might think that after such a disagreeable experience I would have followed my aunt's advice, but curiosity getting the better of discretion I disobeyed her and, selecting a fine evening for the enterprise, set out to the tree.

"As it was two or three miles away, and I was dearly fond of riding, I hired a horse and going along at a jog-trot approached the forbidden spot at about eight o'clock.

"The lane in which the haunted elm stood was narrow, trees of all sorts and sizes lined it on either side, and the shadows, intensified by the thickness of the foliage overhead, almost obliterated the roadway.

"All was dark and silent. I no longer wondered at the villagers fighting shy of such a place; it looked a positive cock-pit of spookdom.

"At about twenty or so yards from the notorious elm my horse showed unmistakable signs of uneasiness, laying back its ears and shivering to such an extent that it was only by dint of alternate threats and caresses that I succeeded in urging it forward. Arriving at a spot level with the tree the animal shied, and had I not been a pretty good horse-woman I might have met with a nasty accident, but I stuck to my seat like a leech, and using my whip smartly drew in the reins. My horse fell back on its haunches; reared—plunged headlong forward—took the bit between its teeth and—we were off like the wind.

"Fortunately I was prepared; leaning back in my saddle I enjoyed rather than otherwise so mad a career. But my pleasure received a sudden check when I perceived, to my horror, the figure of a tall woman dressed in black striding along by the side of us and keeping pace with us without any apparent effort.

"Heaven alone knew where she came from unless from the tree; I fancied I had heard something drop from the branches at the moment my horse shied. As the woman was wearing a cloak drawn over her head, I could not see her face but from the grotesque outlines of her limbs and body, I concluded it must be unpleasantly bizarre.

"We kept together in this extraordinary fashion until we came in sight of Burle, when she quickened her steps, and tearing off the hood thrust her face upwards into mine.

"It was awful—utterly and inconceivably AWFUL—so awful that I felt the very marrow in my bones freeze with horror while my heart stood still.

"She had no hair; her head was round and shiny, whilst her face, yellow and swollen, was covered all over with circular black spots causing it to bear a striking resemblance to one of those old-fashioned carriage dogs!!! Her eyes were black and sinister; she had no nose, whilst her mouth was—horrid—the most horrid thing about her.

"With a diabolical grin she grabbed at my jacket and would, I believe, have torn me from my seat had we not at this moment, in the very nick of time, arrived within sight of the gates of Burle Farm.

"My aunt, with several other people, was awaiting me, and as with a desperate spurt I galloped up to them, the infernal hag let go her hold of my jacket, slackened her pace and vanished."

❑❑❑

CARNE HOUSE, NEAR NORTHAMPTON

THE MAN IN THE FLOWERY DRESSING-GOWN AND THE BLACK CAT

Technical form of apparitions: Phantoms of the dead and possibly animal: Elemental.

Cause of haunting: Murder

Source of authenticity: First-hand evidence

SHOULD any one wonder why I continually select Northamptonshire and Gloucestershire as the scenes of my ghost stories, let me hasten to explain that my reason is obvious enough—with both these counties I have had a lifelong intimacy and naturally have had more facilities and opportunities for collecting suitable material from them than from any other.

I have not the slightest doubt other counties can show equally long lists of haunted houses, only I have not found them so easy of access, moreover the genial nature of the inhabitants of Northamptonshire (especially) has attracted as well as aided me in my research, and although the burly Midland yeoman is inclined to scoff at things superphysical, his satire is not so objectionable as is that of the supercilious middle-class Londoner.

Again, Northamptonshire is very rich in well preserved old country mansions—I know of no other county where there are so many—and as most of these houses have at one time or another witnessed some grim tragedy, it is not surprising that they are now the scenes of occult manifestations.

Doubtless one would find similar phenomena in smaller habitations were the latter of the same early date, for crime was then just as prevalent among the poor as among the rich, but the inferior material with which cottages have been built causes their comparatively speaking early dissolution, and we rarely find a cottage now standing which was built more than a century ago.

From this it must not be deduced that hauntings are confined to old buildings nor that past crime alone begat ghosts; nothing of the sort, modern villas are frequently subjected to psychic phenomena whilst the phantoms of present-day suicides and murderers are decidedly as numerous as of yore.

But whereas in olden times, crime was fairly common in villages, it is now chiefly confined to towns, and the houses that have witnessed murders, &c., are not infrequently entirely demolished or made to undergo some very radical alterations—hence the ghosts disappear with their surroundings.

This more so, perhaps, in the provinces than in London, as there are too many crimes in the latter for any particular one to be remembered for any length of time, not long enough in fact to permanently damn the letting of a house.

The word ghost is very elastic, it may be used in reference to many different types of spirits, and is, in fact, only the designation for that genus of which the departed soul of man is but a species.

Now Northamptonshire is very rich in species; species of all kinds; spirits of men, of beasts, of vegetables! and species of elementals—elemental being in itself, a genus which includes many various types, too numerous indeed, for any attempt at classification in this work.

It is no uncommon thing to meet with some locality (usually barren) or village (generally on the site of barrows or Druidical remains as, for example, Guilsborough) where the nature of the hauntings is dual; a complexity that is, fortunately, of rarer occurrence in houses.

Concerning the latter, Lee mentions one instance, *i.e.*, "The Gybe Farm," in his book, "More Glimpses of the Unseen World" whilst I will take this opportunity to quote another case of dual haunting, *i.e.*, Carne House, which is situated at the utmost extremity of a village to the south-east of Northampton.

My informant, Mrs. Norton, frequently resided in the house in her childhood and youth, and it was from her lips that I heard the following story which I recollect only too well.

• • • •

MY FIRST IMPRESSION of Carne House was one of extreme aversion; I can see it now as I saw it then—vast, sleek, and white, like some monstrous toadstool, or slimy fungus.

Bathed in the moonlight—for we did not arrive till late—it confronted us with audacious nudity; not a plant or shrub being trained to hide its naked sides. There was something unspeakably loathsome in the boldness of its carriage—something that made me glance with fear at its wide and gaping windows and glance again as I crossed the threshold into the dark and lofty hall.

The passages of the house, both in number and sinuosity, resembled a maze; they recalled to my youthful mind the story of Dædalus, and I half expected to see the figure of the Minotaur suddenly arise from some gloomy corner and pursue me through the labyrinth.

Nor were my fears entirely groundless, for I had hardly been in the place a month before I had a very unpleasant experience.

Chancing one morning to go on an errand for my mother to a room that had in all probability once served as a laundry, but which was now restricted to lumber, I was startled at hearing something move either in or on the copper. Thinking it must be some stray animal, or, may be, a rat, I threaded my way through a sea of packing cases, and standing on tip-toe, peeped very cautiously into the copper.

To my intense surprise I found myself looking into a very deep and sepulchral well, at the bottom of which was a man. I could see him distinctly, owing to a queer kind of light that seemed to emanate from every part of his body. He was draped in a phantastic costume that might have been a kimono or one of those flowery dressing-gowns worn by our great-great-grandfathers. He was bending over a box which he was doing his best to conceal under a pile of *débris*, and it was undoubtedly this noise that had attracted me.

Too intent on his work, he was apparently unaware of my close proximity, until, satisfied that the box was well hidden, he straightened his back and looked up.

His face frightened me; not that it was anything out of the normal either in feature or complexion, but it was the expression—the look of evil joy that suffused every lineament before he saw me, changing to one of the most diabolical fury as our eyes met. I was at first too transfixed with terror to do more than stare, and it was only when, crouching down, he took a sudden and deliberate spring at the wall and began to climb it like a spider, that I regained possession of my limbs, and turning round, fled for my life.

Oh! how long that room seemed and what an interminable succession of furniture now appeared to barricade the way.

Every yard was a mile, every instant I expected he would clutch me.

I reached the door only just in time—happily for me it was open—I darted out, and as I did so the outlines of a hand—large and ill-shapen—shot fruitlessly past me.

The next moment I was in the kitchen—the servants were there—I was saved—saved from a fate that would assuredly have sent me mad.

When I related what had happened, to my mother, she laughingly informed me I must have been dreaming, that there was NO WELL there, nor was there any man in the house save my father and the servants; yet I fancied I could detect beneath those smiling assurances a faint and scarcely perceptible horror—and she never let me visit that room again—alone!

But was I dreaming—was there no well, and had that man been but the fancy of a childish and distorted brain?

Sometimes I answered "Yes," and sometimes "No."

After this little incident, a manifest, though of necessity, subtle change took place in our household; the servants became infected with a general spirit of uneasiness, which although only shown in my presence by their looks, convinced and alarmed me far more than any fears, even the most terrible, would have done had they been outspoken. I was positive they lived in daily anticipation of something very dreadful—something that lay concealed in those dark and tortuous corridors or in that grim and ghostly room.

My dreams at night were horrible, nor did I again feel that in this respect I was singular as I overheard some one remark that no one ever passed the night without awakening with a sudden and inexplicable start.

I say inexplicable—would that it had always remained so!

It was August when my next definite adventure occurred. I use the word definite as I had had several other experiences, but of too brief and uncertain a nature to enable me to draw any precise conclusions.

Once, as I had been walking along one of the passages, I had heard the noise of something clanking, and had been put to instant flight by the sound of heavy footsteps echoing suddenly in my rear, and again—but this isn't really worth recording; let me proceed with that night in August.

Well, I slept in a room at the end of a corridor, my nearest neighbour, Miss Dovecot our governess, occupying a chamber some dozen yards away. I do not think I need describe any article of furniture the room contained; every piece was strictly modern, and had been brought with us from a newly furnished house in Sevenoaks. The fireplace and cupboard are, however, deserving of comment; the former was one of those old-fashioned ingles Burns delights in describing, and which are now so seldom to be seen; an inn at Dundry, near Bristol, containing, I believe, the finest specimen in the kingdom; whilst the latter, which I always kept securely locked at night, was of such far-reaching dimensions that it might well be termed in modern phraseology a linen room.

On the night in question, I had gone to bed at my usual time—eight—and I had speedily fallen to sleep, as I was in the habit of doing; but my slumber was by no means normal.

I was tortured with a series of disturbing dreams, from which I awoke with a start to hear some clock outside sonorously strike twelve. As an additional proof of my wakefulness, I might add (pardon my explicitness) I was sensibly affected by a constant irritation of the skin, due, I believe, to a disordered state of the liver, which in itself was a sufficient preventive to further sleep.

It must have been half-past twelve when I heard, to my intense horror, the cupboard door—which I distinctly recollect locking—slowly, very slowly, open.

My first impulse was to make a precipitate rush for the door, but, alas! I soon became aware that I was powerless to act; a kind of catalepsy, coming on suddenly, held my body as in a vice, whilst my senses, on the other hand, had grown abnormally acute.

In this odious condition I was now compelled to listen to the Thing—whatever it might be—slowly crossing the floor in the direction of my bed.

The climax at length came, and my cup of horrors overflowed, when, with an abruptness that was quite unexpected (in spite of the direst apprehension), the Thing leaped on the bed, and I discovered it to be an enormous CAT.

I can unhesitatingly add the epithet—Black—for the room, which a moment before was shrouded in darkness, had now become a blaze of light, enabling me to perceive the colour as well as the outline with the most unpleasant perspicuity.

It was not only in intensity of colour (the blackest ebony could not have been blacker) that the cat was abnormal, but in every other respect; its dimensions were not far removed from those of a large bull-dog, and its expression—the eyes and mouth of the beast were more than bestial—was truly Satanic. Stalking over my legs, its tail almost perpendicular and swaying slightly like the nodding plumes of a hearse, it squatted down between the bedposts opposite, transfixing me with a stare full of malevolent meaning.

I was so fully occupied in watching it and trying to solve the enigma I saw so plainly written in its every gesture, that I did not realise I had other visitors, till a sudden uncertain twitching in the light made me look round. I then perceived with a start a fire was burning in the grate.

A fire, and in August—how incongruous! I shivered.

But it was no delusion; the flames soared aloft, adopting a hundred fantastic yet natural shapes; the coals burned hollow, and in their crimson and innermost recesses I read the future.

But not for long. My cogitations were unceremoniously interrupted by the appearance of the man-in-the-well, whom I was startled to perceive seated in the chimney-corner in the most nonchalant attitude possible—nursing a baby!

Anomalous and mirth-provoking as is such a sight in the usual way, the existing circumstances were grim enough to excite my horror and raise anew my worst forebodings.

Supposing he saw me now? There was no escape! I was entirely at his mercy. What would he do?

I glanced from him to the cat, and from the cat back again to him. Of my two enemies, which was most to be feared? The slightest movement on my part would inevitably arouse them both, and bring about my immediate destruction. The situation did not even warrant my breathing.

The minutes sped by with the most tantalising slowness. The clock struck one, and neither of my visitors had budged an inch—the man in the flowery dressing-gown still nursing the baby, and the black cat still staring at me. Mine was indeed a most unenviable position, and I was despairing of its ever being otherwise, when a sudden transmutation in the man sent a flow of icy blood to my heart.

He no longer regarded his burden indifferently—he scowled at it.

The scowl deepened, the utmost fury pervaded his features, converting them into those of a demon. He got up, gnashed his teeth, stamped on the ground, and lifting up the child, dropped it head first into the fire. I saw it fall. I heard it burn!

The hideous cruelty of the man, the abruptness of his action, proved my undoing. Oblivious of personal danger, I shrieked.

The effect was electrical. Dropping the poker, with which he had been holding down the baby, the inhuman monster swung round and saw me.

The expression in his face at once became hellish, absolutely hellish.

My only chance of salvation now lay in making the greatest noise possible, and I had commenced to shout for help lustily, when at a signal from the man, the enormous black cat crouched and sprang.

What followed I cannot exactly remember, I have dim recollections of feeling a heavy thud and of some one or some THING trying to tear away the clothes from my head, after which there came a very complete blank, and when I recovered consciousness, the anxious countenances of my parents and governess were bending over me.

The next night I slept with my sister.

My health had been so impaired by these encounters, that my parents decided to move elsewhere; the furniture was once again packed, and within a month of the above incident we had taken up our abode in Clifton, Bristol.

The history of the hauntings was subsequently revealed to me by the owner of the house. It had once been inhabited by a man of the name of Darby, who seems to have been a sort of wholesale butcher.

His elder brother dying, the family estate passed to the latter's eldest son, a child of two, and Darby determining to succeed to the property, invited the widow to stay with him. She did so—she was a weakly creature—and he got rid of her by putting her to sleep in a damp bed. The children were next disposed of, the younger by being burnt (as I had witnessed) and the elder, aged two, by being smothered to death by a black cat. Darby is said to have deliberately made the cat sit upon the infant's mouth as it lay asleep. But these rapid deaths, as might have been expected, aroused suspicions. The nurse, who had been an unwilling party to the burning of the baby, turned King's Evidence, and a warrant for his arrest was issued. As is often the case, however, the officers of the law were a bit too late. When they arrived at the house, the quarry had flown, nor could his whereabouts be discovered for many years; not, indeed, till fifty years after the crimes, when his skeleton was found at the bottom of a disused well he had himself sunk in one of the back kitchens. Under the skeleton lay an iron box containing many valuables, rings, &c., which he had been doubtless striving to hide when death in some unaccountable form or another overtook him. What became of the cat, history does not say.

The place had always borne a reputation for being haunted—it was on that account my parents had got it at so low a rental—and the ghosts seen there (undoubtedly those of Darby and his cat) corresponded in every detail with the phenomena that had so terrified me.

I am aware that many deny the existence of souls in animals—let them do so—but do not let them be too dogmatical, for where Life ends all is mystery.

Still there is an alternative theory to account for the appearance of animal phantoms, which is, I think, quite within the realms of possibility: the black cat I saw, if not the spirit of the one made such hideous use of by the old man, was undoubtedly an elemental—a spirit representative of a popular crime, a vice—Darby's evil genius—that ever hovered at his heels in his lifetime and is more loth than ever to leave him now that his physical body is dead and his soul earthbound.

❑❑❑

HARLEY HOUSE, PORTISHEAD

THE BLACK ANTENNÆ

Technical form of apparitions: Poltergeists (or Elementals)
Source of authenticity: First-hand evidence
Cause of hauntings: Unknown

THE following account of a haunted house is taken from the diary of a gentleman—since deceased. The narrator was the owner of the house, and, being a professional man, asked me to give fictitious names, lest the publication of the story should be detrimental both to his practice and to the letting of the place:

"Before I commence my story," he writes, "I think it expedient to state that both my parents are dead, my father having died many years ago and my mother quite recently. The latter had lived to the very ripe age of ninety, had possessed an unusually strong will, was a most devout Roman Catholic, and took the deepest interest in everything that concerned our welfare. She had two peculiarities: (1) A strange aversion to children; (2) a positive loathing and dread of blackbeetles. The house stands alone, some thirty yards or so from the road, and is well concealed from view by a high brick wall and numerous trees.

"There are four bedrooms upstairs, two on either side of the landing—which for clearness I will number—viz., No. 1 occupied by my wife and I; No. 2 my sister Mary's room; No. 3 my sister Joan's room; No. 4 the spare bedroom in which my mother died. The top storey consists of two attics inhabited by the servants.

"January 1, 1906, we first became aware of the disturbances—violent knockings being heard about midnight on the walls and floor of room No. 4. On hurriedly entering it, we could discover nothing. But on leaving the room the noises were repeated and kept up till two or three in the morning.

"January 5. A recurrence of the disturbance—only much louder.

"January 6. Have in a carpenter who makes a thorough examination of the wainscoting and reports 'no traces of rats, mice nor any other animals.'

"January 10. Tremendous knockings again in room No. 4, the door of which is swinging to and fro violently. A loud clatter on landing as though half a dozen children were engaged in the roughest horse-play. The uproar terminates in a terrific crash on the panel of No. 3 door. Joan rushes out of her bedroom thinking the house is on fire and sees a strange, green light some six by two feet long moving across the landing. It disappears in room No. 4.

"January 15. We are all awakened by a loud crash and on reaching the landing find a big, black oak chest from the coach-house, lying there on its back. Every one much alarmed.

"February 1. My sister Mary awakened at midnight by feeling something tickle her cheeks. She puts out her hand to brush it away and encounters something cold and scaly. Her shrieks of terror bring us all into her bedroom—there is nothing there.

"February 3. My wife and I are aroused by feeling our bed gently lifted up and down, and on my getting out for a light, I tread on something indescribably disgusting. It feels like a monstrous insect!!

"February 4. The knocking very bad all night—particularly in room No. 4.

"February 5, 6, 7, ditto.

"February 10. The clothes mysteriously taken off Joan's bed and transported to room No. 2.

"February 15. Both servants undergo our experience of February 3.

"February 16. The knockings still continued and distant sounds heard as of some one coming upstairs and turning the handles of all the room doors.

"February 17. Scufflings on the landings, and in the passage as though caused by a troop of very noisy children.

"February 19. Knockings in room No. 2. The washstand and a heavy mahogany wardrobe moved some feet out of their places. Mary, who was awake at the time, saw the shunting of the furniture, but could detect no sign of any agent.

"March 1. About 8.30 A.M. after Martha had laid the breakfast things she went downstairs to finish a cup of tea. On her return to the breakfast room she found it in the wildest state of disorder; chairs over-turned, ashpan and front of grate removed to furthest extremity of room, all the pictures taken down from the walls and laid face upwards on the floor, and the cups, saucers, plates, knives and forks piled in one heap in centre of table; all this had been done without either breakage or noise.

"Terrified out of her wits Martha rushed upstairs to our door, and nothing would induce her to enter the breakfast room again alone.

"March 3. On returning home about 10 P.M. from a neighbouring town, we found the servants sitting huddled together, half dead with fright in the kitchen. They had heard knockings and the most appalling thuds ever since we had gone out; and on entering our room (No. 1) we found it in an absolute turmoil: the bed-clothes in a promiscuous pile on the floor, the duchess table turned round with its face to the wall, the pictures ditto—but—nothing broken.

"March 15. Awakened in middle of night by three loud crashes in room No. 3, after which we distinctly heard our door open and some one crawl stealthily under our bed.

"We at once lit a candle—no one was there.

"March 18. Knockings in both the attics. The servants badly scared.

"March 21. As Joan was running downstairs about mid-day, she received a violent bang on her back as if some one had hit her with the palm of their hand. She came to my study in a very exhausted condition, and it took her some minutes to recover.

"March 24. Found my mother's shoes, which we were certain had been locked up in a bureau, placed where she had always placed them in her lifetime—*i.e.*, on the hearth-rug before the dining-room fire.

"March 31. My mother's favourite arm-chair found upside down in front of the fire-place in room No. 4.

"April 2, 11 P.M. As Mary was stooping to look under the bed for fear of burglars, she was suddenly pushed down and the mattresses and bedclothes were thrown on the top of her. Her frantic struggles and muffled screams being, fortunately, overheard by my wife (I was in London at the time), she was immediately extricated. No injury, only bad shock.

"April 3, midnight. The contents of a large chest of drawers in room No. 3 suddenly emptied on to the floor. Loud crashes in all parts of the house.

"April 10, 11 P.M. On going up to bed, we find room No. 4 aglow with a pale green light and filled with a faint sickly odour, which we at once recognised as identical with that smelt there at the time of my mother's decease and which we considered was peculiar to her disease.

"I must mention that after her death, the room had been thoroughly renovated, the old flooring replaced by new, the walls repapered and everywhere well disinfected with the strongest carbolic. My mother had died at 11 P.M.

"April 12, 13, 14, 15; 11 P.M. The same light and smell.

"April 20. Joan fell over some large obstacle in the hall, hurting herself badly. She could see nothing, but was half suffocated with a stench similar to the one already described.

"April 30, 2.20 A.M. Both my wife and I distinctly felt something brush across our faces. We lit a candle and perceived to our horror two long black antennæ (like the antennæ of a monstrous beetle) waving to and fro on our pillow.

"We spent the rest of the night on the drawing-room chairs and sofa.

"May 1. Shut up the house."

NOTE.—An attempt to solve the mystery surrounding these hauntings will appear in a subsequent volume.

❑❑❑

THE WAY MEADOW, SOMERSET

THE INVISIBLE HORROR

Technical form of haunting: Unknown
Source of authenticity: Personal and other experiences
Cause of haunting: Unknown

IN my boyhood days I was very fond of making long excursions on foot, my peregrinations taking me many miles from Bristol, which was at that time my home. On one of these occasions I took a route that led me past Bath, and eventually arrived at a village that particularly fascinated me.

Lying in a hollow by the side of a sluggish river, or stream, it presented an exceedingly attractive appearance to my somewhat romantic eyes. I especially liked the whitewashed cottages, with their thatched roofs, diamond-fashioned window-panes, walls and trellised arches covered with jasmine and Virginian creepers; their tiny gardens crowded with foxgloves and roses, and their quaint, their very quaint chimney-pots, from which arose spiral columns of fleecy-looking smoke.

It was a pretty village, a pre-eminently peaceful village; a village that was rendered almost fantastic by the close proximity of a queerly constructed water-mill; it was a sunny village, remarkably hot in summer, but intensely cold in winter.

The stream to which I have alluded ran its tortuous course through a succession of open meadows. In the corner of one was a pond, a deep and silent piece of water that was supposed to be connected in some way with the miniature river. It struck me as a very proper place for a bathe, the weeping willows that fringed its margins affording an effectual screen to the prying eyes of children; whilst the gently sloping banks of spongy grass were softer to the tread than any towel.

To add to my inducements the sun was unusually hot, which made the thought of a bath very tempting after my long tramp over dry monotonous roads.

Plunging in, I was, however, immeasurably surprised to find that, despite the abnormal heat, the water was icy cold, and that the scalding rays from above did not appear to have the slightest effect on the temperature.

Taking a few rapid strokes, I found myself nearing the opposite bank, and was preparing to turn about when a sudden panic seized me, and, fancying I was being pursued, I scrambled ashore.

Seeing nothing, and consequently assured that my fears were due to the trickeries of imagination, I once again entered the water and was well on my return voyage when I experienced the same sensation. I seemed to feel the presence of some extremely hostile and repulsive body—something that lived in the pool and bitterly resented intrusion. So strong was this feeling that I would not on any account have bathed there again—at least, not alone.

In response to my inquiries in the village, I learned that the meadow, which went by the name of "The Way," bore a very evil reputation, being carefully avoided by the local people after nightfall. Though nothing had been actually seen there, those who had attempted to cross the field in the dusk emphatically declared they were assailed by an "invisible something" that was indescribably cold and horrid, and that they only escaped from it after the most strenuous exertions.

Nothing short of force would induce a dog or a horse to enter the meadow, and farmers fought shy of letting their cattle graze there; indeed, should any farmer be so foolish as to do so his beasts invariably died.

I suppose I looked a trifle sceptical at this, as the blacksmith remarked: "Don't smile, sir; if you saw Way Field, and especially the pool, after twilight, you would form a very different idea of it to what you do now. In the day-time it is, as you see, all sunlight and daisies, an ideal spot for tea in the hay; but in the evening the aspect undergoes a complete change. The temperature is invariably lower there than it is in any of the other meadows, whilst the shadows that crowd upon the grass are not in the least representative of any trees! Curious, sir, is it not?"

I readily agreed it was curious, and I was so deeply impressed by all that had occurred that, years afterwards, when chance once again brought me in the district, I lost no time in setting off to visit the pond.

To my astonishment it was gone, and its site was now occupied by the kitchen garden of a large house, evidently the abode of some person of means.

I made inquiries and had but little difficulty in obtaining an introduction to the owner who was not only acquainted with what I already knew, but was able and willing to give me further information, with the stipulation, however, that on no account must I mention either his name or that of the locality. He wanted, he explained, to sell the place and he could not hope to get a fair price for it, if the story of the hauntings appeared in print.

"I have been here three years!" he began, "during which time I have had no less than eight housekeepers and twenty-five servants (my usual staff consists of four); that signifies a good few changes. Eh?"

"Yes, it has been a confounded nuisance!" he went on, "none of them would stay on account of the ghost! I pooh-poohed the thing at first, although I honestly felt there was something very queer about the place, but when one after another came to me with the same yarns, I was obliged to admit there might be something in it.

"Their complaints, though differing slightly in small technicalities—due, perhaps, to their unequal descriptive powers—were on the whole co-incidental; frightful dreams, sudden awakenings without any apparent cause, strange creakings on the staircases, the foot-falls of something soft and indefinable, the rattling and turning of door handles, and over and above everything else the most pronounced feeling of insecurity.

"'I won't on any account remain downstairs after the rest have gone to bed,' one of my housekeepers observed on my asking her to sit up for me, 'the very first night I stayed here—before I had heard any rumour of the place being haunted—I underwent the most unpleasant sensations on being left alone. I instinctively felt some uncanny creature had begun to walk the house as soon as the lights were out. No, sir. I am ready and anxious to fulfil all my other duties, save this, and if it is really indispensable, why I fear, sir, you must get someone else in my place.'

"This I promptly did, but all to no effect. The newcomer had not been with me a week before she approached me with a very woe-begone face.

"'I am sorry, sir,' she said, 'I must give notice. I am by no means nervous, indeed I have always laughed at ghosts, but there is something unmistakably the matter with this place, especially the garden!'

"'The garden!' I exclaimed, 'Come, it's the first time I have heard there's anything amiss with the garden.'

"'But not the last, I'll warrant you,' she remarked caustically. 'Why sir, unless I am very much mistaken, the origin of the disturbances lies in that garden, over there,' and she shot a bony forefinger (why should housekeepers invariably have bony fingers?) in the direction of the filled-in pond. 'As I was gathering some lettuce there last night I felt (I could see nothing) some horribly cold and sticky thing clasp me in its arms. It must have been hiding among the raspberry canes. Struggling with all my might I managed to free myself just as a mass of fetid jelly was closing over my throat and mouth. Oh! how desperately I struggled, and what a blessed relief it was to be free from that loathsome presence. I can assure you, sir, I ran across the garden as fast as any girl, nor did I pause for one second, till Johnson and one of the maids came to my assistance. They did not ask me what had happened, bless you sir, they knew! Nor was a word said about it at supper, no one dare even as much as mention the thing by gaslight!'

"It was useless, Mr. O'Donnell, to try and persuade the woman to remain with me after THAT, she went and, by the bye, I have just heard she has recently undergone an operation for tumour in some provincial hospital.

"With my next housekeeper I was rather more fortunate. She stayed with me for more than six months before showing any of the usual signs of restlessness.

"Then she came to the point without the least embarrassment, springing her surprise on me over the breakfast cups.

"'I must leave!' she said demurely, proceeding at the same time to pour out the coffee, 'there is a certain dampness here that is very trying to one subject to rheumatism, as well as to one's nerves.'

"I started guiltily. 'A dampness! Nerves! you astonish me,' I stammered, 'pray explain yourself.' She did so.

"'What I mean is,' she observed, 'that I can never enter the lower part of the kitchen garden without being persistently followed by a "mist"—I should have put it down to mere imagination, had I not accidentally heard some one speak about the ghost, and I at once concluded that the mist must in some way be connected with it—am I not right?'

"Of course I assented—what else could I do?

"'I thought so,' she went on demurely, 'I suppose you do not think it necessary to tell your applicants the place is haunted?'

"I shook my head feebly and muttered: 'Continue.'

"'Last night,' she said, 'the mist was more pertinacious than ever—it not only pursued me in the garden, but came to my window after I had gone to bed. I was looking at the moon when the temperature of the room suddenly fell to zero, the moonlight blurred, and to my amazement I saw the mist clinging to the window-pane. Mr.

——, I am not a nervous woman as a rule, but I wouldn't stay in this house another month under any conditions.'

"She went—and once again I had to go through all the bother of advertising. The wretched thing now began to haunt more vigorously than ever. It attacked Emily, the cook, on the kitchen staircase, and Mark, my general factotum, in the stables, both leaving in consequence, and both being afterwards taken very ill. Indeed it was the report of their illness that prompted me to wage war against the ghost—if I had to leave the house, it should not be till I had ascertained something more definite about my enemy. I would try and discover its identity—what it actually was! With this end in view I laid every trap imaginable, my ingenuity being at length rewarded by finding a faint and barely perceptible impression on the surface of a very large tray full of a carefully prepared mixture of gelatine and wax. I had placed the tray in one of the passages usually frequented by the EVIL PRESENCE. On examining the impression under a powerful microscope I fancied I could detect innumerable granules composed of radiating threads with bulbous terminations.

"Elated at my success and wondering very much what it represented, I took a photograph of the impression and sent it to a medical friend—a bacteriologist—in London, whom I knew to be interested in psychical research. In the course of a few days he came to see me, and, pointing to the wax tablet, remarked:

"'I showed the photograph you sent me to some of my colleagues, and we came to the conclusion that the impression bore a distinct likeness to a number of actinomyces, which, as you may know, are a kind of fungi inimically disposed to every kind of animal—cattle in particular. Indeed they are in the main responsible for one of the most common and deadly bovine diseases which is called actinomycosis, and is acquired by cattle eating infected barley or other cereal, the actinomyces adhering to the tongue or jaw.

"'In man the disease is very similar in its clinical character and may be caused by a number of organisms belonging to the streptothrix group (I fear this is rather too technical for you) forming colonies in the tissues and obtaining access to the body from a carious tooth or not infrequently from the tonsil.

"'The disease is sometimes wrongfully diagnosed as tuberculosis; it usually occurs in farmers, millers, and others who are brought in contact with grain; it has a tendency to spread locally, and although not dangerous in itself, may become so by attacking important organs or by becoming generalised, thereby giving rise to pyæmic abscesses in all parts of the body.

"'In the description of the assault on your housekeeper, to which you gave special prominence (and rightly so) in your letter, you mentioned that the EVIL PRESENCE tried to "get at her mouth"—well that would be in strict accordance with the *modus operandi* of actinomyces, the primary endeavour of which is to obtain a passage through the lips. Furthermore, you gathered from local gossip that the unfortunate woman had undergone an operation in some provincial hospital for tumours; now tumours are usually one of the sure indications of the nature and progress of the disease.

"'Lastly, you referred to fatality in any cattle allowed to graze in the haunted meadow. Now you know from what I have already told you that cattle are the favourite victims of the fungi.

"'From these deductions then, one must inevitably arrive at the conclusion—that the haunting here is due to nothing more or less than the phantasm of a giant mass of ACTINOMYCES—and as this type of spirit would undoubtedly be proof against exorcism my only advice to you is to shut up the house and go.'

"Afterwards, with a view to corroborate my friend's theory, partly for his satisfaction, partly for my own, I am afraid, Mr. O'Donnell, I agreed to rather a cruel thing—the proposal being that we should experiment on one of our dogs—Spot. Turning him loose in the lower extremity of the garden, we took up a position in the loft of a neighbouring barn, where we clearly saw each act in the grim but exciting drama.

"To begin with, Spot did not at all appreciate being left alone. From the very first he manifested distinct signs of uneasiness, his preliminary barks of disapproval speedily changing to those of fear and culminating in howls of positive terror, as tucking his tail between his legs, he careered madly round the enclosure.

"He did not, however, keep up this pace for long, but soon showed unmistakable signs of flagging, coming to an abrupt halt sooner than we had expected.

"The Evil Presence had, we felt sure, got hold of him.

"Thrust back on his haunches and snapping viciously, his eyes protruding and his mouth foaming, poor Spot presented such an appearance of impotence and terror that I rose to interfere and would doubtless have done so, had I not been persuaded to the contrary by my medical friend, whose professional interests he either could not or would not sacrifice for the sake of sentiment.

"Poor Spot eventually died, and our *post mortem* pointed to ACTINOMYCOSIS—his body being literally perforated with abscesses.

"Thus you see, Mr. O'Donnell, in discovering the identity of the phantasm I accomplished—in part at all events—my purpose; the cause of the haunting must, I am afraid, remain a mystery."[5]

❑❑❑

NO. — HACKHAM TERRACE SWINDON

THE GHASTLY SCREAMS ON THE STAIRCASE

Technical form of apparition: Phantasm of dead
Cause of hauntings: Unknown

LAST December I journeyed up from Cornwall, as usual, to the annual concert given by my old school, Clifton College, and at the subsequent House Supper I made the acquaintance of several O. C.s who were considerably my juniors in point of age.

We chatted together for a long time, and in the course of our conversation touched upon the superphysical.

"You couldn't have a better authenticated instance of a haunted house," one of my young friends remarked, "than that of No. —, Hackham Terrace, Swindon. Isn't that so, Neilson? You come from Swindon."

Neilson agreed.

"I know the people who live there," my informant, Jarvis, continued, "and they have seen and heard the phantasm over and over again."

"What form does it take?" I asked.

"A shrieking woman's."

"Like the ghost of Tehiddy," I ejaculated.

"I have never heard of the ghost of Tehiddy," Jarvis rejoined, "but I cannot conceive anything more gruesome than the Hackham Terrace apparition. Let me tell you some of Mrs. Belmont's experiences.

"You must know the house is quite new, the Belmont's being the first tenants, and that nothing has been discovered, so far, that can in any way account for the hauntings.

"To proceed, about a month after they had taken the house, every one was aroused in the middle of the night by a succession of the most unearthly screams, coming, so it seemed, from the basement of the house.

"For some seconds no one ventured out of their rooms, and then, Mrs. Belmont very pluckily taking the lead, other members of the family followed her down-stairs.

"Arriving at the commencement of the passage leading to the kitchen, they all saw an indefinable black object lying on the ground.

"Frozen to the spot with horror, the Belmonts watched the thing slowly rise, developing as it did so until it assumed the appearance and dimensions of a gigantic naked woman. But what was so inconceivably horrid about her was the face: she had no eyes, their places being filled by ordinary flesh.

"Confronting them for some moments in silence, she suddenly and without the least warning assumed a horizontal position in mid-air, dematerialised, and passed through the wall in the guise of a rectangular mass of pale blue light. Could anything be more ghastly?"

"It has parallels in the luminous woman known as Proctor's ghost, Wellington, near Newcastle, and in a house, also new, in Portishead. Can you tell me any further experiences there?"

"Yes," Jarvis rejoined; "one of the servants was breaking coal in the cellar one evening, when the hammer was unceremoniously snatched from her hand, the candle blown out, and a blue, tatooed arm thrust so roughly against her face that one of her front teeth was actually loosened.

"She screamed, and the arm vanished.

"Still another incident: One of the Belmont boys, Percy, was preparing to get into bed one night, when something caught him sharply by the foot, and looking down, he saw to his surprise a large hairy hand encircling his ankle.

"He particularly noticed the nails, which, though filbert in shape, were excessively long and dirty.

"Mumbling a prayer, the first that came into his mind, he emphasised it by a violent kick. He could not say which produced the desired effect—the prayer or the kick—but the hand let go its hold, and the next moment a shapeless mass of blue something rising from the bed, and hovering for the briefest duration of time on a level with his eyes, disappeared through the ceiling.

"On another occasion, when Mrs. Belmont was in the conservatory watering flowers, one of the pots behind her suddenly fell to the ground with a crash.

"She turned round and found herself confronted by a blue face that occupied the spot where the pot had stood.

"Too dismayed and startled even to think of escape, she stood rooted to the spot, gazing at the evil thing in open-mouthed horror. What was it?

"Though resembling a man in contour and features, its expression was too thoroughly bestial to belong to anything human.

"The eyes, deep, sunken and lurid, leered malignantly at her, whilst the mouth was distorted into a diabolical grin.

"The apparition had no body.

"Mrs. Belmont is of the opinion she might have stayed there till doomsday had not the unexpected arrival of the gardener scared the thing away—it disappeared as he entered the greenhouse door and its place was once again taken by the flower-pot!

"Mrs. Belmont had another unpleasant experience only this week.

"As she was crossing the landing to her bedroom one morning, some one seized her by her shoulders, and, pulling her violently backwards, threw her on the floor.

"She was then gripped by the throat (so firmly that the impressions of the fingers could be seen next day), and on looking up she encountered the same awful face she had seen in the conservatory.

"The hateful thing was now in full possession of a body which, blue and hairy, accorded well with the strangely animal expression in its eyes.

"Mrs. Belmont was too fascinated and horror-stricken to struggle, and she thinks she would undoubtedly have been strangled had not succour once again arrived at the most opportune moment.

"Her rescuer this time was Bruce, a very pugnacious Irish terrier.

"Nothing daunted, and contrary to what one is led to expect from the generality of psychic tales, Bruce flew at the figure.

"The phantasm immediately dissolved into a blue vapour and vanished.

"I could enumerate many other occasions on which similar occult phenomena occurred in the house; sometimes the eyeless woman would be seen gliding down the staircase or heard screaming in the passages; at other times the blue man would pounce upon his unsuspecting victims out of some dark sequestered corner, or frighten them to the verge of a fit, by simply peering at them through a door or window—the manifestations always terminating in a bluish vapour."

"The house, you say, was quite new," I observed.

Jarvis nodded.

"Then the history of the hauntings," I replied, "must either be in some piece of furniture or in the ground itself. The blue man with the bestial expression in his face and tatoo-marks on his arms suggests to me the probability that he is a phantasm of an ancient Celt.

"Possibly he was a suicide or murderer; possibly he was neither, but is merely tied to this earth by his animal propensities—in either case, he would hover round the place of his burial, and his naturally ferocious spirit would be rendered doubly ferocious at being disturbed.

"The woman, of course, may have been some one associated with him in this life—the lack of eyes the sign of some dreadful depravity in her nature."[6]

❑❑❑

APPENDIX TO NO. — HACKHAM TERRACE, SWINDON

AT Jarvis's request, I related to him the story of "The Screaming Woman of Tehiddy," taken from a collection of remarkable narratives on the certainty of supernatural visitations from the dead to the living, impartially compiled from the works of Baxter, Wesley, Simpson, &c.

I chose this tale as the least hackneyed and best authenticated of the many accounts I had heard of similar occult phenomena. It is given in the original text, the extracts being taken from the letter of one "S. W." to his friend "Charles."

"I had occasion one day," he writes, "to visit the hamlet of Barnley, some miles distant from Tehiddy, where I was staying with some relations. My stay was unexpectedly prolonged till a late hour, and having promised to be at home before night, I was compelled to set out on my return much after the period at which it ought to have been commenced. Part of my road lay through a thick and lonely forest, and I confess that the task of traversing it would have been more agreeable at an earlier opportunity.

"My spirits were affected from some indefinable cause, and the chill, dark journey I was preparing to take did not tend to raise them. I swallowed a hasty cup of coffee with my friend, shook him cordially by the hand, and mounting my horse, was soon at a considerable distance from his house.

"I was approaching the verge of the forest, and had just entered a narrow outlet from it, when I heard the roll of distant thunder and felt the wet and heavy droppings of a copious rain. Having scarcely a league farther to travel before I reached home, I determined to urge my horse to the utmost, and escape, if possible, by his speed, from the impending storm. He broke at once into a gallop, when I struck him with the spur, but had scarcely gone a hundred paces before I was thrown from the saddle by his abrupt stopping, and pitched with the greatest violence to the ground. I lay stunned for a few moments by the fall; the first thing that brought me to a sense of my situation was a *hoarse scream*, uttered by some person who breathed close to my ear. The rein, which I had continued to grasp in falling, was at that moment torn violently out of my hand—I heard the noise of my courser's hoofs as he started back—the scream was repeated, and something rushed past me that clanked as it went like a horseman's heavy iron-cased sabre. I sprang up from the earth and threw out my arms to ascertain if any individual were actually passing; but the avenue was so narrow that I touched the hedges on each side of it, and felt instantly convinced that nothing human could have gone by. A recollection now flashed upon me that there was a tale of extreme horror connected with this part of the forest, and in spite of the principles which I summoned to my aid, it was in a mood of mingled desperation and amazement that I reflected on the circumstances with which my memory supplied me.

"The infirmary of Tehiddy, about twenty years ago, contained a female patient who was known by the name of Martha, and had been admitted to that asylum at the instance of a stranger. He stated himself to be her husband, and assured the director of the institution, with the appearance of the deepest sorrow, that she laboured under a lunacy of the most stubborn sort, which nothing but the most severe discipline attributed to his house was likely to abate.

"He advanced a large sum for the maintenance of this unhappy creature, saw her lodged in one of the strongest cells of the establishment, and, having recommended an unsparing use of the scourge, thought proper to depart. His meaning was not misunderstood. The shrieks of poor Martha were heard day and night in the vicinity of her dungeon, and suspicions soon prevailed that she was being sacrificed to the cruelty of her merciless keepers. An investigation of the case was proposed by some humane and spirited people, but a calamity of the most awful kind put a stop to their endeavours. Martha was found dead on the borders of the forest, at the very spot I have described to you, a piece of ragged iron being clenched in her grasp, with which she had torn and gashed her throat in a dreadful manner. The escape of this wretched being was never well explained, and hints were dropped that she had not left the prison alive. Her bloody and mangled remains excited a strong sensation among those who inspected them. Marks of the chain and the whip were conspicuous on every part of her body, and long tufts of her thin grey hair were glued together by the stream that had issued from a deep fracture in her head. The tokens of suicide, however, were undeniable, and the remains of the poor maniac were in consequence buried near the place where they were found.

"This occurrence had scarcely ceased to be the subject of conversation, when the whole town of Tehiddy was agitated by events of a yet more appalling character. *Hoarse screams* were heard in the still dark hours of night, and a pale bloodless face was seen pressing against several of the chamber windows. Fraud or delusion were naturally suspected in a business of this nature, and the most scrutinising inquiries were made into the evidence on which it rested. No detection took place, and the screams soon became so frequent that not a person continued to question their existence.

"It was midnight when I reached home, exhausted by anxiety and fatigue, and, being provided with a key to my apartments, the people of the house had not waited up to receive me. I drew off my boots and upper coat as a preliminary to the act of undressing, and seated myself in a large antique chair, from which, when divested of my clothes, I usually stepped into bed. Here I fell asleep owing to excessive weariness, and may the next slumber that is likely to end in so horrible a way be never broken.

"A dream was upon me full of blood and death; the shrieking maniac flitted through my brain in a thousand forms, and seemed, at one time, to stand over me brandishing a sword of fire.

"The next moment, I lay benumbed, as it were, in my seat, while the maniac advanced from a dark corner of the room, bearing in her right hand a human skull replete with some poisonous sort of drink. This horrible potion was lifted to my lips, which seemed to shut in vain against it, the long, bony fingers of the phantom being thrust into my mouth, so as to force a passage for her accursed mixture. It trickled down to my very heart in slow, cold drops, and when lodged there seemed, by a sudden transition, to burn and glow like flames of Etna; spellbound as I was, such extreme agony passed my powers of endurance. I uttered a frantic cry and sprang up from the chair, darting towards the hag by whom my torment was inflicted. The glare of her red eyes grew stronger as I advanced, and a lean, sallow arm was put out to repel me. Fearing the detested touch, I hastily drew back; some article of furniture intercepted me; I fell, and was plunged from the fall into a chasm, which opened through the floor. The shock of this awoke me, and the first proof I obtained of my actual perception was the sound of that *hoarse scream* which a few hours before had been uttered in the forest. This scream was repeated—it seemed to issue from the windows. I heard the casement flap, as if a strong wind were shaking it; and though my sinews shrank and withered at the noise, yet I staggered to this window as fast as my feet would carry me. A ray of light flashed in as I reached it, and there, pressed close against the glass, I saw the same pale, bloodless visage that has been already figured to you.

"Maddened by the sight, I clenched my hand and drove it fiercely at the apparition.

"Its lips quivered—the *scream* rang again through the apartment. I was found next day without sense or motion, my hand dreadfully cut, and the window shivered to pieces."

❑❑❑

PARK HOUSE, WESTMINSTER

THE CAVALIER'S GHOST

Technical form of apparition: Phantasm of the dead

Source of authenticity: Miscellaneous collection of Ghost Stories by Baxter, Wesley and Simpson

Cause of haunting: Murder

(The following story is told *ad verbum* in the language of the eye-witness, the quaintness of his style being accounted for by the period in which he lived.)

"I was always a very strong-minded man, and, until the time about which I am going to speak, always ridiculed the idea of ghosts.

"You must know that about two years ago[7] I went to lodge at an ancient house in Westminster, where nothing remarkable happened to me for about three months; and then, on a night in November (too well do I remember it), I saw such an appalling sight as I never before beheld.

"Even were I starving to-morrow, I would not again enter that room—no, not for a thousand pounds! I had been to the theatre, and on my way home had drunk a single pint of porter, so that no doubt of my sobriety can exist for a moment.

"My room was on the second storey of a house that, I should suppose, had weathered well-nigh four hundred years, and was in former days an isolated habitation.

"The room, surrounded by a wainscoting of oak to the height of five feet, was very lofty, and even in the lightest days, owing to the narrowness of the windows, was extremely gloomy. As I said before, I returned from the theatre, and the snuff of the candle, which I had extinguished on getting into bed, had not ceased to emit its disagreeable effluvia when I beheld—my blood freezes when I think of it—a young man, dressed in the habit of days gone by, gliding through the wainscoting on the opposite side of the apartment to where I lay.

"I was completely paralysed—trembled violently in every limb—and the perspiration fell in torrents from my brows.

"I felt for some time as if every nerve was cut asunder and every sense benumbed.

"I exerted myself to speak, but in vain; my tongue cleaved to the roof of my mouth, and I was obliged to remain a horror-stricken and inactive spectator of the scene before me.

"The apparition remained for nearly ten minutes, which was ample time for me to convince myself that it was no idle chimera of a diseased imagination that stood before me. Yet although it remained so long a time, I could not command sufficient resolution to challenge it or summon any one to my aid—for I felt as though deprived of all energy, and, in fact, I was so during the whole time of its visit, though my sense of perception and consciousness were painfully acute.

"The expression of the countenance was peculiarly mild, and the rich dark locks falling about the forehead and shoulders, and the mustachios of the same hue, showed in horrid relief against the ashy, chilling, and livid hue of the face.

"He wore a doublet of a kind of chocolate colour, richly embroidered with gold lace, full loose breeches of a yellow leather, ornamented uniformly with the doublet, and from each was suspended a bunch of ribbon, adorned with a metal tag, reaching down nearly to the broad and drooping tops of his light russet boots.

"A large travelling-cloak of dark blue cloth reached from the shoulders down to the heels, hanging in full folds over the left arm, which was extended towards the fireplace of my apartment.

"While I was gazing on him in stupid astonishment and terror, he raised his right hand, and lifting from his head his broad, sable-feathered hat, discovered to my agonising sight a deep and bloody wound in the centre of the forehead.

"This action he then followed up with sighs and gesticulations which, although I could not clearly understand, were apparently intended to warn me of some impending danger.

"Harrowing as the sight was to my feelings, it was a mere nothing to what I suffered when I beheld him advance, slowly and almost imperceptibly, towards the spot where I lay, and fixing his dark, piercing gaze upon me for nearly a minute, hold me in a more painful and horrid inactivity than that in which the basilisk is said to hold its victim.

"Although I knew from the expression in his eyes he wished me to speak, and much as I desired to hear from him some of the mysteries attached to the superphysical world, I could not articulate a sound (a phenomenon which I have since learned invariably happens to psychists at the crucial moment).

"At length he retired towards the wainscot, and raising both his hands in the attitude of prayer, remained apparently wrapped in deep contemplation for nearly three minutes, and then suddenly disappeared—sinking into the floor at the bottom of the wainscotting. As you may well suppose, I did not close my eyes again that night, but as soon as it was light I proceeded to my landlord's room, roused him, and demanded to settle my account, for I determined in my own mind never to re-enter the house which was visited in so superhuman a manner.

"With astonishment in his countenance, he received the amount of my rent, at the same time inquiring what had caused this sudden aversion to my apartment.

"I answered evasively, and as I left him I thought I observed a kind of lurking consciousness of something wrong in his countenance, which led me to surmise he was fully aware of the mysterious visits of the apparition; and so it proved in the end, for, happening to meet him one day in the park, I inveigled him into confessing that it was reported in the neighbourhood that the house, and particularly the room in which I slept, was haunted by the troubled spirit of a young cavalier of King Charles the Second's days, said to have been murdered there. 'And,' he added, 'during the time he had kept the house, no less than nine people had left the apartment on account of the disturbances. He had concealed this from me,' he concluded, 'fearing I might add one more to the list of lodgers scared away by the supernatural vision.'"

□□□

GLOSSARY

ELEMENTAL. Otherwise known as Poltergeist. There are too many species of this genus of spirit for me to attempt a classification in this work. Broadly defined, an Elemental is a phantasm that has never inhabited any kind of earthly body whether animal or vegetable. It may be sub-human, as in the case of the Clock-ghost of Mulready; sub-animal, as in the case of the Guilsborough apparition; or sub-vegetable, as in the case of the ACTINOMYCES phenomenon near Bath.

It is generally, but not always inimically disposed towards man. One type of it, viz., the gnome, pixie, &c., avoid humanity as much as possible; other types are merely mischievous, delighting to frighten children by visiting their nurseries or pouncing out upon them when at play in some deserted building or lonely by-road; whilst other species are wholly evil, generating bacilli of foul diseases or urging man to the commission of vicious acts and crime. Their origin I reserve for another volume.

GHOST. The general name for phantasms, &c.

HALLUCINATION. Any supposed sensory perception that has no objective counterpart within field of vision, hearing, &c.

CLAIRVOYANCE. The faculty or art of perceiving some distant scene as though an actual eye-witness. A clairvoyant is often able to describe (unconsciously) what he is witnessing.

DELUSION. Fancy. When one imagines one sees or hears something and it exists ONLY in imagination. Hallucinations are either delusive, when there is nothing to which they correspond in the objective world, or veridical, when they correspond with events taking place somewhere.

ILLUSION. Misinterpretation of some object actually present to the sight, as, for example, when a cloak hanging on a peg is mistaken for a man, or a ringing in the ears for sounds of bells.

METETHERICAL WORLD. The world beyond the ether, synonyms—spiritual, superphysical.

PHANTASM. A ghost. Any occult phenomenon that is either visual or auditory as distinct from a phantom which is only visual: or, indeed, any superphysical presence that conveys the impression of touch, smell, &c.

SUGGESTION. Process of impressing upon a person's intelligence or mind the thoughts and wishes of another intelligence or mind; or ideas engendered by the appearance of certain localities, furniture, &c., or simply by the atmosphere.

[1] In the March number of the *Psychical Research Magazine* for 1908, a well-authenticated instance is given of a Poltergeist's hand being seen on a pillow—"a long hand with knotty joints."

[2] A solution as to the nature of this type of ghost will appear in a subsequent volume.

[3] All names altered by request.

[4] The different styles of writing in the following are due to certain alterations I have been obliged to make, the English of the original being so involved in places as to be nearly unintelligible.

[5] In a subsequent volume I have attempted to give a satisfactory solution.

[6] A more thorough solution to these hauntings will appear in a subsequent volume.

[7] (Probably 1780.—ED.)

www.ingramcontent.com/pod-product-compliance
Lightning Source LLC
LaVergne TN
LVHW092047010426
835292LV00009B/484

9789361440328